I0747529

Beaujolais Blood

An unputdownable puzzle of a cozy mystery

Christa Bakker

Counting Blessings

Contents

1

I thought you were supposed to be good at it

I opened my eyes and screamed. Not that the sight was so hideous, but I had not expected the face of my assistant hovering over me when I woke up. His name was Thibault but everybody called him Beau, for very obvious reasons. Handsome as he was, I still didn't want him to be the first thing I saw in the morning.

Thibault staggered back, apparently also not expecting this reaction from me. He recovered quickly, however, and thrust my phone in my face.

'Julie, keep your... your' – he swallowed a swear word, which I appreciated – 'phone with you. The thing has been ringing for ages. Woke me up at this indecent hour.'

I glanced at my smartwatch, which I now realised was vibrating almost violently. Eight o'clock. I narrowed my eyes at him. 'How did you get in?'

He shrugged, rubbing his eyes and yawning while he made for the door.

I sat up, bunching the duvet over my chest. 'Thibault Fouquet, how did you get in?! I'm sure I locked the door last night.'

He turned on a dramatic sigh. All blond youthful innocence, he spread out his arms. 'So I picked the lock. You have the worst security around here. You should really do something about that. What if they steal your cameras?'

'You know how to pick locks?'

'Are you really surprised?'

Come to think of it, I wasn't. His family and I weren't exactly on the same side of the law. That didn't mean I couldn't glare at him now for putting his dubious skills to use on *my* back door. He belonged in the room above my studio. Actually, though he'd been in there for the past month and a half, I still wasn't sure he belonged there or anywhere else on my land.

'Thank you for the phone. Now go back to your side of the property.' I tried to make my voice sound icy, but he didn't seem impressed. To top off my frustration, my phone chose that moment to start ringing again. It was my brother. Too unawake to keep the phone to my ear, I put him on speaker.

'David, what is the emergency that you're calling me about at eight in the morning? And by that I mean there had better be an emergency.'

'I broke my ankle and lost my house key. Can you come and collect me from the train station?'

'Right.' I blinked to process whether this should constitute as an emergency. 'How did you...' Skiing. Good morning, brain. Thank you. He was on a skiing holiday. 'Never mind. Let me get dressed and I'll be there as soon as I can.'

I hung up and dropped the phone on the bed. Then I fell back and turned over, pulling the duvet up to my chin.

'You're supposed to go pick up your brother.' Thibault fled my bedroom when my pillow came sailing at his head.

Twenty minutes later, my brother folded himself into the passenger seat of my car. I closed the boot and joined him in the front, turning the heat up high. The predicted early snow hadn't fallen yet, but everything pointed to it coming.

'I thought you were supposed to be good at it,' I couldn't help teasing.

He grunted, not dignifying my taunt with an answer. I supposed it must be hard for the golden child to have something not go perfectly in his life. Though I was successful in my business, in my family I was just the girl taking pictures of other people's bums. Yes, I'm a pin-up photographer, but the tasteful kind. No nudity, just 'Whoops, did my skirt fly up?'. Sass, baby! I love it.

But my family loves it less. Except maybe for my great-aunt, whose house I now own, and of course my mum, because she's my mum, everyone looks down on my chosen profession. The Belmains are an old and distinguished family and we do not lower ourselves to this kind of standard. You should hear my uncle go on about our history and the time we had ties to the British court.

Sometimes I wish my dad was still alive. He was about the only one who understood me. But then, if he hadn't died, I wouldn't have rebelled against my family and married a man whose sweet side reminded me of my dad but whose dark side took over as soon as we were married. Long story short, he's doing time for fraud and I'm spending time trying to fall back into favour with my family.

This tall-dark-and-handsome next to me, however, is a whole other story. Twenty-nine – two years younger than me – a paediatric surgeon, never been married, never been divorced, always done everything by the book. Naturally, he's completely un-standable. For normal people, that is. My family can stand him and then some. But then, our family is pretty much the golden family in our village of Saint-Maurice. Probably one of the reasons why I still haven't felt at home there since I came back.

David stared out the window for the ten-minute drive back through the undulating Beaujolais countryside. With the bare vines ready for winter, the vineyards always looked as if they were bracing themselves. 'If we can get through this unnecessary cold patch, we can start again in spring,' they seemed to say. Was I projecting my own feelings onto them? Very well possible! Why don't humans hibernate? Nobody wants their pasty complexion captured for posterity, so my business wouldn't suffer. But then there's people like David, who actually seek out the cold. Just so they can break their ankle.

He was still silently staring. This was nothing out of the ordinary, though. Our lives were so different that we didn't have much to say to each other. Usually. Today, I wished he'd at least tell me about his holiday.

As I got back in the car after opening the big metal gates to his drive (because why would you modernise?), I ventured a question. 'So how were the slopes?'

'Tricky.'

'*Ça alors*, you are grumpy.'

'What did you expect? I was supposed to be out there, having fun with my friends. Instead, I'm hobbling into my big empty house, and Anne is probably cosying up to Yohan right now.'

That, I was sure, brought a glimmer to my eyes. 'You were showing off? For a *girl*?'

His jaw muscles tightened. He'd said too much and knew I was not going to let this go for a long time. So childish, I know. But this was my perfect brother. It was my duty as his elder sister to point out every flaw he showed.

But when he hauled his surly face out of my car, took his crutches from the back seat, and made an attempt at dignified hobbling, I took pity on him. My brother lived in a big, centuries-old house overlooking the village, full of stairs and thresholds. All by himself. How was he going to cope with all those obstacles on crutches? I rounded the car and shoved my shoulder under his arm. Since he was quite a bit taller than me, I was an easy support.

'Thanks,' David mumbled.

Built in the eighteenth century by Joseph Belmain, La Grande Maison resembled a child's drawing of a house – a rectangle with a bunch of windows and a triangle for the roof. Except the triangle had its tip cut off and the proportions were massive. The golden yellow stones so common to the region had been smoothly cut, contrary to the rough stones most houses were made of. Though I wouldn't want to live here all by myself, knowing that the house was still in our family always filled me with a sense of pride.

Entering through the side door so David wouldn't have to climb the steps to the entrance, I led him through a little corridor to the kitchen, where he sank down on a chair.

'So... do you have something like a guest bed to set up downstairs?'

'I'll sleep on the couch.'

'All right, I'll make you some coffee and then I'll bring down some bedding.' And some clothes. Ordinarily, he wouldn't be caught dead wearing joggers outside of the gym, but jeans weren't going to fit over that cast.

He nodded, and I set to work in silence. His cupboards were almost empty, which shouldn't have surprised me. But I remembered these cupboards from when we came here at Christmas as kids. The cupboards were always overflowing then, though now I realised that must have been the case only at Christmas. My great-uncle had lived here alone, much like my brother now did.

Leaving David with a steaming mug, I went upstairs but then realised I didn't even know which room my brother used. I opened a few doors, all of them leading to dusty rooms filled with sheet-covered furniture – some antique, some just old. While I knew David wasn't here for much more than sleeping, the sight of La Grande Maison in such a state of disuse brought a sadness to my heart. Not much I could do about it, though. David was always either working or out with friends in Villefranche or Lyon. I guessed not many of them wanted to come all the way out here.

At last, I located David's bedroom and went downstairs via the grand staircase in the hallway. This, at least, was dust free. The carvings on the bannisters showed the opulence this villa had once displayed. The house had been built around 1750 but had survived the Revolution more or less intact. Much of the gilded glamour had since faded, though, or been traded in for more modern conveniences. I say *more* modern, because the last change to the house and its interior had been right after the Second World War. And then only to eliminate every trace of the Nazis who had occupied it on the invitation of that family member whose name shall never more be mentioned. See? I wasn't the only one bringing shame to the family. But in a weird way, I took courage from this guy. At least I wasn't as bad as him.

By the time I'd made up a bed on the couch in the salon and joined David in the kitchen, I'd also made a phone call.

'I've hired you a temporary domestic helper.'

His eyebrows lifted, then fell. 'You've what? I don't need help. I just need to heal.'

'There's no food in the house and there are steps everywhere. How are you going to keep it all clean over the coming weeks?'

Glaring at me, he opened his mouth for a retort that stuck in his throat.

'She'll be here this afternoon. Her name is Maëline, and you are going to be nice to her.'

'I'm always nice,' he growled.

'Right. Call me if you need me.'

'I won't need you. But... don't you want some coffee or something?'

I paused at this unexpected display of civility. Tempted to accept, I then saw us just sitting here, staring at each other. 'I still have to put my face on.'

He peered at my face. 'But you're wearing make-up.'

'This? This is nothing! Bare minimum for emergencies.'

He threw his hand up in defeat and hid his face in his mug.

For once, I thought some show of affection might be in order, so I put my hand on his shoulder. Let's not go crazy. 'I'll go get you some breakfast. Anything else you need?'

'No. Thanks.' It sounded so sad that I really felt for him then.

'Be right back.'

2

Child minder

Snow clung to Maëline's brown hair as she climbed the steps to the mansion. La Grande Maison was aptly named. It looked like a regular house, only much bigger. Pulling the cord, she could hear an old-fashioned bell tinkle on the other side of the door. Adjusting the backpack on her shoulder, she hoped her patient wouldn't be put off by the size of it. Though it was normal for a live-in helper to bring a good-sized bag, circumstances had made hers... a bit bigger than usual.

After about an age, the door opened to reveal a handsome, dark-haired man under a thundercloud.

'Hi. I'm Maëline. I've come to help you?' She had, of course, come to help him. But she'd found that if you let people confirm that fact from the get go, it eased them into accepting the help. With this tactic, paired with her naturally soft voice, she could often convince the most stubborn patients to yield. This was the first time she'd taken a live-in job, though. She'd had to.

'You'd better come in. It's cold.'

That it was. Much like this reception. What had the sister said when she called the agency? He was a doctor, so he knew he'd need help, but he didn't want it. 'Too clever for his own good', she'd called it. In other words, arrogant. Why send her, then? He'd probably be better off with a child minder.

Thundercloud sighed. 'I'm David. My sister called you in, but I don't think you'll have much to do. It's just me, and I'm often away.'

Classic. 'I'm not here for the house, I'm here for you. If you need to go out, I'll go with you.' Expected glare received, she continued, 'I assume you're not going in to work, so that's a chunk of your time you'll be spending here instead. Any other activities I should know about?'

He grunted, turned to lead her into the house but then turned back to her. 'Look, I told my sister I don't need you. I can't help you and I haven't prepared a room for you. You'd better leave. I'll pay you for the time lost.'

'That's all right, those are exactly the kinds of tasks I'm here to help you with. And I've already been paid, so I might as well stay and be of use.'

'I don't want to be rude' – too late for that, she thought – 'but I don't want you here.'

See, child minder. That's what he needed. If only she *could* leave. She pretended to give in, dropping her shoulders and looking defeated. 'Well... would you mind if I had a drink of water first? Or maybe a cup of tea? I've come all this way, and it is quite cold.'

He seemed happy to grant that request with the prospect of her leaving. Without the scowl, his face was actually quite pleasant. Huh. He led her to the kitchen, fumbling with his crutches as he held the door open for her.

'You should disable that door closer. It's just going to be in your way.' Yes, she could do it, but then he wouldn't know he'd needed her for it.

David looked at it, half turned to the door, then realised he was holding his crutches and grumbled, 'I'll do it later.'

Maëline parked herself on a kitchen chair, demurely waiting for her tea. Watching David lean his crutches against the counter and cursing under his breath when one slipped and fell to the ground, she wondered how long it would take for him to get over himself and ask her for help. And what if he didn't? Her outward show of defeat threatened to leak inward. It had taken all her determination to go ahead and take this job, but if it fell through, she had nowhere left to turn.

For now, David left the crutch where it had fallen and filled the kettle. Leaning against the counter, he managed to pull the tea from the cupboard above. But then, he'd already done this wrong once today. In the corner, the broom hid a pile of coffee grounds. High cupboards and low drawers. No one who's suddenly on crutches expects them to become the bane of their existence. But if you only have one working foot and you need both hands for something, it's easy to fall over. No, he really didn't need her.

Tea ready, David turned around to put the mugs on the table and promptly tripped over his fallen crutch. Maëline shot up. She caught him before he got hurt but in doing so got in the way of the tea sloshing over the edge of the cup. Clenching her teeth through the pain of the hot tea soaking her clothes, she stabilised David and then frantically pulled her top out to let in some cool air.

David frowned. 'Are you all right? Do you need some cream?'

No apologies. Interesting. Tucking in her chin to blow down her top, she held up her hand. 'It's okay. I would like to change my clothes, though.'

'Of course.' Putting the tea on the counter, David bent down to get his crutch and promptly toppled over. He cursed loudly and swatted at Maëline's outstretched hand. 'All right, you win! Stay if you want, just don't get in my way.'

Maëline would have smiled with relief and a small amount of victory if her chest hadn't burned so much. She manoeuvred him onto a kitchen chair, dragged another towards the door, and fixed the door closer. 'Since you've so graciously accepted my help, I'd like to take my things to my room.' Her soft voice took most of the sting out of those words, but she was pleased to see David's eyes narrowing. She needed the job and therefore had to keep her client happy, but he should learn to be more civil. Stepping down, she picked up the crutch. 'Unless you need me for something else?'

'*Non.*' Then after a pause, he added in a more cordial tone, '*Merci*. You can take any of the rooms upstairs, but I'm afraid they haven't been used in a while.'

She nodded, grabbed her rucksack, and headed back to the hall and upstairs over the polished stone steps. Admiring the ornamental pillars and oil paintings along the walls, she slid her hand over a carved figure of Mary in a little alcove. Dust clung to her fingers. Hm, if it turned out that David really didn't need her all that much, she'd still have plenty to do here to earn her wages.

After having located David's bedroom, she chose the one next door to set up her own camp. Lifting a few of the sheets to reveal a white wooden bed with beautiful flowing lines on the headboard and a matching vanity unit, she whipped out her phone and took a picture. *Think I'll be all right for a few weeks*, she texted the friend who'd let her crash on the couch.

She replaced the soaking top with a cream-coloured shirt and a chunky knit charcoal cardigan, which didn't go as well with her asymmetrical skirt, but they'd do. Before she went back downstairs, she allowed herself half a moment to sit on the edge of the bed and take a few deep breaths. It was good to be back at work, but the work itself seemed to have changed. To be around someone who *didn't* want her help was refreshing. She remembered all the tricks from before, but they felt different now. Making someone want her help raised all kinds of conflicting emotions in her, letting her know that she was far from over her ordeal, but she was determined to get there.

Talking to her new host was the first step. She found David in the living room, reading a book on the sofa that had been made up as a bed. He looked up when she entered, his face showing signs of guilt.

'I'm, err... I'm sorry I acted like a... so grumpy. I know you're just here to help. I guess I was annoyed with my sister for calling you and I took it out on you. Have you found everything you need?'

Maëline nodded. 'I'd like some fresh bedding, but I'll do that later. Anything I can do for you right now?'

'I'm all right. Didn't manage to bring your tea, though.'

She smiled. For a split second she wanted to tell him she'd only asked for tea to make him see he did in fact need her. If he turned out to be a nice guy after all, why not be frank? But maybe admitting to deceit was not the best way to start this off. Despite his pleasant expression, these were the first decent words he'd spoken. Besides, he could easily kick her out of his house after all, and then where would she be? Until he got used to her, it was probably best to keep her thoughts to herself. 'That's fine, I'll get it myself.'

Drink in hand, she settled into one of the old-fashioned armchairs. 'So what happened?'

'Skiing.'

Oh-kay. Back to the single-word answers. Although this time he shifted, as though he wanted to say more, he still remained silent after the one word.

'Shame,' Maëline continued. 'Your garden would be a perfect slope when it snows. Although a bit short for skiing. I bet the kids love it for sledding, though.'

'I wouldn't know.' He glanced out the window with something of a reminiscent look.

'Oh, you haven't lived here long?' Maëline had spotted some unpacked moving boxes under the stairs, though somehow David and the house seemed to fit together. Stiff and formal, but comfortable with their position.

He didn't answer at first, but moved his hand as if in search for the right words. 'My family has owned this house for centuries. I only took it on because my sister and I are the last of the line, and she didn't want it. Something about our great-uncle dying here. It's far too big for me, of course, but my mother would kill me if I sold it.'

Maëline shivered. Given the age of the house, the great-uncle probably hadn't been the first to die here, but the thought alone made the skin on her arms tingle.

'We grew up coming here for Christmas and other celebrations, but sledding in the garden would never have crossed our minds.' He huffed a laugh. 'The frivolity! No, these were solemn occasions. Not gloomy per se – we laughed and had a good time – but there was never any silliness. And sledding would have been regarded as such.'

'Maybe, next time it snows, you could open the gates and see what happens.'

All he did was raise an eyebrow, and she figured the topic was closed. Outside, the gate gave a metal groan.

'Ah, that'll be my sister.'

3

You're a woman of the world

'Watch out!'

The warning came too late, as I looked up the moment a load of snow slid off the roof and hit my head. Every muscle in my body froze, almost literally. A young woman came running from La Grande Maison to the abandoned buildings at the bottom of the garden, while I stood there, half covered in snow, holding my grocery bags.

The woman, who must be the help I hired for David, stretched out her hand to take my bags. '*Tiens*, let me take those. Are you all right?'

Her soft voice full of concern, she put down the bags and reached for my hand. Only then did I move to shake off the snow and step out of the pile at my feet. 'Thank you. Yes, I think I'm okay. It took me by surprise, that's all.'

I shivered, now starting to feel cold trickles underneath my coat.

The young woman looked up. 'I wonder where it came from. There isn't all that much snow built up yet. Not enough to drop by itself. Strange…'

It *was* strange. I'd only veered off the path towards the empty buildings because I thought I'd seen something move inside. But whatever it was, I didn't care about it any more. I wanted to get inside and warm up, so I grabbed one of my bags and legged it to the house. The woman gave the roof one more glance, then picked up the other bag and joined me.

'I'm Maëline, I've come to help your brother?'

I smiled around my chattering teeth. 'I thought as much. Julie.' I would have offered her my hand, but I needed it to keep my coat closed around my neck.

Maëline nodded in acknowledgement.

'How is he? Has he been awful to you? He doesn't mean to be, he—'

'He's… had to accept my presence.' She grinned.

I slowed my pace in surprise. That was quick. It usually took David a lot longer to admit defeat. I had a feeling Maëline and I would get along quite well. I grinned back at her but turned away to open the door and let us both in.

'I can't stay long because I have a client at ten, but I've got you a few essentials – *du lait, quelques oeufs…*' I took the milk and the eggs out of the bag to demonstrate, but Maëline stopped me.

'I'll do that in a minute. Let me make you some coffee first. You must be so cold.'

Ah yes, this girl I liked. With my fingers wrapped around a steaming mug, I complimented her clothing style. That romantic, earthy vibe was something I could never pull off but I did love it on others. It suited Maëline perfectly. She had an almost elvish quality to her, with her soft voice, fair skin, and finely carved features. But the fact that my brother had given in to her presence spoke to an underlying firmness of character.

We chatted for a while, until I realised I'd told her all about me but still didn't know anything about her. She knew about my flight to the city in the valley, Villefranche, when I was twenty-two. She knew I got married and divorced, set up my business, and fled back to Saint-Maurice. She knew about Mum being the latest in a long line of village mayors, and that I thought David would take over someday. She now knew everything about me but *she* was still a mystery. Hm. That didn't happen very often.

When my mug was empty, I felt warm and dry enough to brave the weather again. It was only a short drive anyway, since I'd left my car here when I walked to the village for some groceries. I hopped into the living room to tell David again to be nice, which annoyed him no end, of course. When I came back to the kitchen, whom should I find but Thibault, perched on the corner of the kitchen table, trying to impress Maëline, who looked about as unimpressed as an architect examining a Lego model.

'Ah, Julie! I was on my way back from the *boulangerie*, so I thought I'd walk home with you.'

'The time you spend at the bakery, Céline should start asking rent. Right, let's go then. I want to get out of these wet clothes before the client arrives.' I pushed Beau out the door, wished Maëline good luck, and closed the door behind me.

Thibault frowned. 'Wet clothes?'

I related what had happened when I returned with my groceries.

'But... why were you over there?' He gestured towards the empty buildings that stood well to the side of the entrance. Ordinarily, anyone walking up to the house wouldn't go near them.

'I thought I saw... Well, never mind. It must have been a stray cat or something. I heard a noise on my way out and when I came back, there was movement inside, so I went to check it out. Dumb idea.'

I got in the car and drove out while Beau closed the gates behind me. I should really talk to David about modern conveniences. Beau chatted about something or other on the way, but all I could think about was that my underwear was getting damp from the melted snow seeping into my clothes.

I pulled into my driveway at the same time as Maile, my make-up artist. Whatever the weather or the circumstances, you could count on Maile to be there exactly ten minutes before the client's appointment.

'Last one, eh?' she called out as she got her luscious Hawaiian curves out of her car.

'Mmm-mm. One more to get through.' I locked my car and let her into my studio through the glass door.

'Oh. Not a good one?' She wrinkled her nose, but even doing that she looked gorgeous. Her wavy black hair hung thick around her shoulders and with her love of flowery, figure-hugging skirts and tops, she was about as perfect a pin-up as any in my pictures. But her skirts never had a mind of their own. They did exactly what she wanted them to. And that's why she also created most of my wardrobe, personal and professional.

I shrugged, pulling a jumper in my size off the clothing rack. 'What's good? But I prefer it when I'm making a difference in someone's life. When they come in shy and unsure if this is actually what they want, but they leave with a huge smile after a life-changing experience – *that* is what I'm doing this for. This one, though...' I hesitated.

Today's client was a local woman who'd recently moved to the village. Whereas most of the villagers wouldn't be able to afford me, to her a session's worth was pocket money.

Her husband was always at work, leaving her to spend what he made. In her fifties, wearing designer clothes made for teenagers, she spent her days volunteering, which in her case meant making sure everyone knew what charities she'd donated to. She saw this session as 'supporting the local economy'. No lives would be changed today. I worked my way out of the wet jumper and into the dry one.

Maile nudged my arm with hers as she marched past me, hips swinging. 'Hey, guess what? La Tisseuse is happening! My own clothes shop! I got the grant and I'm already planning. It's a good thing you're off work, because I have so much to do...'

She stopped abruptly, a slight panic in her eyes. She'd been talking about this for months – planning, budgeting, and applying – but no matter how well-prepared she was, the uncertainty of her future endeavour still got to her. I hugged her to congratulate her on receiving the grant but had no time to elaborate before my client pulled up.

Teetering on sky-high heels, Sandrine Lardy breezed into my studio. '*Coucou!* Good to see you, *ma petite*. Shall we get started? I presume you remember what I wanted? *Merci, p'tite.*' She said the last bit to the dressing room as she draped her heavy coat over my shoulder in passing.

One, two, three, four... I got to nine before I'd gathered enough humility to hang the coat in its rightful place. When

I entered the dressing area to ask if she wanted coffee, she was already in Maile's chair.

'So I heard you're doing free sessions for locals?'

I was taken aback for a moment. With all her money, was she looking for a freebie? 'I... was *trying* to catch a murderer.'

'Ah, yes, I heard how your little efforts helped the police. Good for you. Must have helped your business, though, giving out free sessions?'

'It was just the one session, and I did it for a friend.' Well, Marie had become my friend afterwards, once all of the unpleasant business with two murders in the village was behind us. The free session had been my ploy to catch a killer, but it had landed me a friend instead. 'Would you like a coffee, Sandrine?'

'Oh no, *p'tite*, I only drink spring water with cucumber. And I have my own.'

Very well, then. I left Maile to deal with Sandrine and took a moment to remove some excess negativity from my head. I'd started doing this a few years ago and kept it up since it seemed to work. Putting my forefinger and thumb together, I pressed against my temple until I could imagine whatever it was that was bothering me being sucked out as if by a magnet. Then I pulled, holding the imaginary thought-filth between my fingers until I could deposit it where I wouldn't be reminded of it. This time it went out the window of my office.

I closed the window and did my rounds to check that everything was set up for the poses Sandrine had selected. In colder weather, the pool and the little stream at the bottom of my garden were out, of course, but my early winter appointments would have a choice of Christmas-themed poses. However, as it was only mid-November, Sandrine had chosen 'Hold the Phone' and 'Out to Dry'.

Thibault was stoking the fire in the corner of the room. Though 'Out to Dry' was never the first pose we did, as it required the client to strip, we always made sure the room was nice and toasty. Not that many clients went for a pose that had them act as if they'd taken an accidental dive with their clothes on. The picture had them covering themselves with a towel and warming by the fire, while the clothes dripped in the background. But even for the women who jumped at the chance to have a cheeky picture taken, going the full monty, if only in the studio and not in the picture itself, was a step too far for most. But it was the first pose Sandrine had picked.

Apparently I sighed when I adjusted one of the lights because Beau mumbled, careful not to let the sound travel through the open-plan studio, 'Not in the mood today?'

I dropped my hands to my sides. 'Is it that obvious? I'd better take some acting lessons or something.'

'You *could* leave this one to me?'

I glared at him. He'd been interested in learning about photography and had already picked up a lot, but there was no way I would leave him to do a whole shoot any time soon. 'Beau, you're twenty-one. Not old enough to be left alone with my clients.'

'I'm twenty-two.' It came out rather sulkily.

'Really? I thought you were ten years younger than me.'

'No, you're nine years *older*. And anyway, age shouldn't have anything to do with this.'

'Exactly.' I turned, feeling his daggers in my back. Strangely, though, putting Beau in his place made me feel better. 'Are you ready, Sandrine?'

With new determination to give even the already overconfident client the experience they were paying for, I complimented Sandrine on the way she looked. This was always a sincere remark because even when clients didn't feel the transformation, their beauty came through once Maile was done with them. Sandrine went straight to the couch and draped herself over it, legs in the air. Her head upside-down over the seat, she suddenly spotted Beau and froze.

I looked between my client and my assistant. He wouldn't have... would he? I knew he had a bit of a reputation for being a Don Juan, but... 'What is it, Sandrine? Would you prefer to keep this a girls-only session after all?' I always asked my clients this ahead of time. Hardly anyone minded the presence of a man, but I had sent Thibault out before.

'No, no, it's fine. Proceed.'

Quickly checking in with Thibault, I saw him shrug and hold up his palms, so I handed Sandrine the pink cord-phone I'd found at a *vide-grenier*, a flea market, that summer and dutifully clicked away. Whatever she had felt when she laid eyes on my assistant had apparently evaporated.

Sandrine took directions surprisingly well, and seeing her pictures turning out better than expected, I regained some of my usual enthusiasm. When it was time for her to take her clothes off for the next shot, I asked if she wanted me to send Thibault away, but she looked at me like I was crazy. Beau, of course, only grinned, but even he hid his face behind a reflector screen when she started stripping right there and then. Maile hurried in with the big towel to cover Sandrine and set to work on wetting her hair, while Beau and I exchanged a look.

Shrugging off any more thoughts about Sandrine's behaviour, I engaged social mode and asked her if she had plans for the evening while she looked so good.

'Not so much tonight. I think I'll need to catch up on my beauty sleep before the Beaujolais Nouveau festivities.'

Ah yes, the third Thursday in November, when the arrival of the first new wine of the season was celebrated with pomp and circumstance. Fireworks, concerts, tastings, communal meals, walking tours... No expense was spared to make the celebrations of the region's raison d'être more spectacular than the last.

'Oh? Going anywhere special, or is the village *caveau* holding the event of the season?' Every village around here had their own wine bar. Naturally, they joined in the festivities, but I couldn't see Sandrine settling for a local party.

Sandrine let out something between a giggle and a cackle. 'Oh, Julie, you're hilarious! No, the Vicomte de Montmalè is holding an extravaganza for the 750th anniversary of his *domaine*, his wine estate.'

'Montmales,' I corrected her automatically. It was something non-locals always got wrong, not pronouncing the last *S*. Montmales was the next village up the hill. Technically, it was on the next hill over, but the valley between the two was so shallow that everyone considered it to be a dip in the same hill. Though the village itself was even smaller than Saint-Maurice's 1,200 inhabitants, it boasted a beautiful old castle, surrounded by one of the largest vineyards in the Beaujolais area.

As the young viscount was one of my brother's best friends, I'd heard about his big party on Thursday but I hadn't given it much thought. I did not move in the same circles as my brother. I usually went to Villefranche for whatever seemed like fun on the day of the Beaujolais Nouveau, but today was only Monday.

'Sounds good. Are you looking forward to it?'

'*Chérie*, they say it's going to be spectacular!'

I smiled, but as Maile had finished, I guided Sandrine over to the fire and continued the shoot. Somehow, though, being nude had also stripped away her ability to follow directions.

'You're supposed to look surprised, Sandrine. Perhaps a little cheeky. But' – duck face is not attractive – 'the come-hither look doesn't suit this style of picture.'

'Sorry, I'm used to doing this kind of stuff for men.'

'For your husband, you mean?'

She fluttered her eyelashes at me. 'Pssh! Come on, Julie. In your profession, you're a woman of the world.'

I was beginning to be. You wouldn't believe the things people tell you when they're comfortable enough showing you their underwear. Hiding my face behind the camera, I hummed. The session ended with Sandrine dropping the towel extra low, making for a picture I might delete but was sure she'd buy if I didn't.

Thibault retreated upstairs to his own studio, and Sandrine immediately leaned towards me.

'Thibault Fouquet? You and Beau?'

So that's what had struck her before. 'No, not me and Beau. Not like that.'

She leaned back, seemingly half disappointed, half relieved. 'I did think! You know...'

The implication irked me. 'What?'

'Well…' She bobbed her head from left to right. 'He just… has no standards, you know? He always seems to go for the most desperate. Figured you would not be that person yet.'

'What do you mean "yet"?!' One… two… three… It wasn't working. 'And Thibault has plenty of standards. Even if they may not be ones that you see.' I should stop talking. I had no idea what Beau's standards were. Why was I defending him anyway?

'All right, all right.' Sandrine giggle-cackled again, holding up her hands in defence and almost dropping the towel completely. 'I see how it is. Forget I said anything.'

Last client, last client, I chanted inwardly. *Two weeks off, just one more client.*

Somehow, I made it through the wrap-up without more outbursts and even managed to be cordial by the time we said goodbye. But as soon as she'd left, I plonked down in the comfy chair in Maile's domain. This woman-of-the-world needed recharging.

Thibault came to find me after saying goodbye to Maile.

Getting up, I narrowed my eyes at him. 'You knew, didn't you?'

'Knew what?'

'That Maile's grant had come through. I told you I'd want to know whether I needed to find a new make-up artist and you didn't say anything.'

He held up his palms. 'I'm innocent. Or at least, I was sworn to secrecy. Do you believe that? Otherwise, I just wasn't interested enough to tell you.'

I whacked his arm. 'You need to figure out where your loyalties lie. Remember, I provide both the roof over your head and your salary. I expect some gratitude in the form of juicy gossip.'

'You know I love you, Juju. That's why I keep things from you for your own good.'

He swaggered across the little courtyard to my house. Closing the door to my studio behind me, I bit the inside of my cheek. Now why did that statement ring so true? Sometimes I felt like the whole village was in on some secret they wouldn't share with me. Though I'd grown up here and my mother was the mayor, I hadn't felt like one of them since I ran off to Villefranche. Even after my return, it had been them and me, not us. While Thibault had been a constant almost from the moment I came back here, whenever he said things like that, I felt more alone than ever.

I entered the living room and switched on some music. I'd already turned towards the kitchen to join Beau when I stopped. Something was off. I turned back and looked around, but it still took me a while to find the empty spot on my wall, where last time I looked there had been three old keys from my collection, framed and hung – not two.

'Who wants to be a millionaire, have busty crumpets everywhere,' Thibault sang 'along' to the music. 'Hey, isn't that out of your time?'

I frowned at the wall one last time, making a mental note to investigate the missing key later, then joined him. 'Don't put me in a box, little boy. But for your information, this song is from 1956. Peak pin-up time, if you ask me.'

Not having won this one, he changed the subject. 'What are you doing, then, with your all-important time off?'

I let my hand flutter about. 'Oh, you know. Things to do, people to see.'

'In other words, you have no plans.'

'No set plans. Marked difference there. I've loads of indefinite plans. I'll probably go see Tiana...' I trailed off, disappointed with the fact that I could only come up with the one indefinite plan.

'And?' Thibault urged.

'And none of your business!' There, I showed him. 'Groceries and stuff too. I might go to the boulangerie.'

He huffed. 'You go to the bakery every day.'

'Not true.' I held up my finger. 'I usually send you.'

He bobbed his head in acknowledgement and emptied his coffee cup. 'Glad to see you have a full life ahead of you.'

'Like you're all that much better. It's your first time off since you came here. You should be... I don't know. Not here.' So much for the pretty speech. But he'd caught me off guard. I rearranged some of the tins and jars on my kitchen counter, annoyed that his grumpiness was getting me down. Now I'd have to make plans just so he couldn't make fun of my useless time off. 'It's not useless,' I said out loud, more to myself than to him. 'Sometimes I need some time without clients, to recharge. Get my thoughts together. Make plans for the new season.'

'I thought you said you did that in February because nobody wants to have their picture taken when they're pale and wintery-faced.'

'Well... yes... but the autumn is busy season, and I get the blues too when the days are getting shorter. When I'd just started this business, all I did was work. Be glad you weren't around that first winter because nobody deserved to see that side of me. I ended up offering the few clients I had that winter a reshoot. It was that bad. Next year I took the two weeks off and I never looked back. So don't get in the way of my relaxation, you hear!' I was shaking my best mum-finger at him, but he took no notice.

'Now I wish I had made some plans. Didn't think you'd go through with taking the time off. What d'you want for *déjeuner?*'

'Err...' was my intelligent answer. What was he doing making assumptions about my decisions? He was getting far too familiar with me, waltzing in here in the morning, drinking my coffee, and fixing me lunch. Then again, I couldn't really mind that, could I? He was good in the kitchen. He'd make someone a lovely cook someday. Still, though that someone was me for now, he should realise that this position was temporary. This was my place. Until he showed up, my man-free place. By choice. He'd essentially robbed me of that choice. Sure, you could argue that I'd chosen to let him stay, but only because he... well...

'Why don't you go see Tiana, and I'll get the groceries and make us some lunch.'

That! See? That's what he does. He just makes a decision, and it seems so reasonable that I can't really argue with it. Utterly irritating!

'No.' Ha! I'm the boss around here. 'Let's have lunch at Jeanette's.'

'If you're paying.'

'When am I not?'

'*Allons-y.*'

4

This was very, very inconvenient

Perching on the corner of her bed, Maëline brushed her hand over the freshly changed covers. Things could be worse. Her phone buzzed with a text. *I won't miss your snoring. Appointment with landlord tomorrow. Will ask if he has anything free.* Maëline fired off a quick thanks. With a little bit of luck, she wouldn't need a new place for another few weeks. It would give her time to save up for the deposit. Dropping down on the mattress, she closed her eyes for a minute.

A little bit of luck? She'd need masses of it to convince this guy to let her stay that long. He seemed okay with her for now, but soon he'd get the hang of his crutches, and she'd be out. She opened her eyes and let her gaze wander around the room. It was unfair. He had all these rooms he wasn't even using, and she had to worry about where she'd sleep when he kicked her out. She sighed. No use getting bitter about it, though. She had a job to do if she wanted to stay here for at least a few more days.

Raising herself on her elbows, she stared at her backpack. Would it be worth unpacking? Maybe she should, for the mental impact if not for anything else. Show her subconscious that she intended to stay here. David had told her to make herself comfortable after all. This room would help with that. Maëline loved the *ton-sur-ton* whites and creams, the ruched sheer curtains, and the soft velvet on the chair and ottoman in the corner. It was a woman's room. A happy woman's room.

What a contrast to next door, where David slept. She'd opened the door earlier, when she was looking for a room to claim, but as soon as she'd established that this was David's bedroom, she'd closed the door on all its darkness. How could he sleep there and not be affected? But then, maybe he was. Despite his initial grumpiness, he did not seem to be the origin of the bad vibes in that room, so maybe the grumpiness was the result of it.

Try telling that to people, though. She'd learned early on not to talk about her feelings of places. Very few people shared them or even believed her. Funnily enough, they would accept it if she said a room felt happy, but if a space had an eerie feel to it, the reaction was almost invariably a waving of hands and a long and low, spooky 'Ooooooh!'. Apparently, people had to make fun of her when she pointed out negativity, whether they felt it or not. So she'd stopped pointing it out.

Maëline got up off the bed. She'd unpack later. For now, she wanted to do a bit more exploring. All the rooms on the first floor opened onto a landing big enough to house a billiard table and have room left for bookcases on either side. The staircase was at the back, meaning the first door you passed coming up led to David's room. Maëline had taken the next room, leaving five more doors on this floor alone. And then there was another floor above this one, plus the downstairs and the souterrain she had yet to see. So much to discover!

However, after viewing one dusty room after another, she soon lost the enthusiasm to continue exploring. In the end, she grabbed her tablet and joined David in the living room, where she asked him for the Wi-Fi password.

'So I can log my hours, *tu vois*?'

David nodded and swung his legs off the couch, but she stopped him.

'No, please, stay there. I can get it. Just tell me where.'

He frowned but didn't comment other than to direct her to the sticker with the password code inside the cabinet that concealed both the TV and the Wi-Fi hub, as well as a number of gaming consoles. Maëline grinned at his selection of games. It seemed they shared a preference for racing games.

'Have you found everything you need?' David asked.

'Yes, thank you.'

'Anything else I can do for you?'

She smiled her most subservient smile. 'I'm here to do things for you, remember?' The instruction that came through the agency had been to 'be firm with him when – yes, when – he causes trouble, and tell him not to do stuff', giving Maëline some good insights into both the brother and the sister. The sister seemed like fun. Couldn't pass a reflective surface without checking herself. What was her name, Julie? She'd heard them talking in the other room, before that Thibault came into the kitchen. The frustration Julie had triggered in her brother was hilarious. If only Maëline didn't need his roof so badly, she'd have been tempted to tease him about it. He was obviously used to getting his way, and a broken ankle probably made him mad at his own body for not conforming to his wishes. 'So is there anything I can do for *you*?'

He shrugged with a half-smile. 'I can't work, and all my friends are on holiday. I think I'll just sit here and read. Through there is the study. You'll find it doubles as a library.' He indicated a door behind him.

'Oh, I'm... not much of a reader. I like to keep busy.'

Another shrug. 'Suit yourself. I won't mind if you'd rather go into town. I can always call you if I need you.'

Except he wouldn't. 'You might want my number for that.' While they exchanged numbers, she asked, 'So what do you do?'

'Paediatrician.'

'Kids?'

His eyes twinkled at her surprise. 'Unexpected?'

She shrugged one shoulder, trying to cover up. 'There's nothing here that hinted at your profession.'

Nodding, he stared at the floor. 'Children should never be sick. I do what I can to get them out of that hospital as soon as possible. So, in a way, I spend my life sending children away from me. That must be why they leave no trace.'

Wow. That was about as laden a sentence as she'd ever heard, but she chuckled at his attempt at levity. 'How long have you lived here?'

'About a year.'

'Really?' Oops, that came out way too incredulous. From the unopened moving boxes in his study, she'd gathered the move would have been quite recent. On the other hand, the kitchen cabinets held cans that should have been thrown out months ago. She'd wondered when she'd found them whether he'd moved with his out-of-date cans or if they were the dead uncle's. Somehow, she couldn't forget about him. One of the rooms upstairs had felt unnaturally cold. She bet herself that's where he died. That, or David's bedroom, depending on whether he'd been sad or evil.

David narrowed his eyes. 'Yes, really. Why?'

'Oh, it's just...' Oh dear, now she was blushing. At least he'd have no trouble believing she'd do whatever he told her to. Perhaps it would secure her place here. 'The boxes. In the study. If you haven't needed those things in a year, why would you keep them?'

He snorted. 'Look around you. I think I can afford to store a few things I don't use every day. Sometimes...' A wistfulness filled his voice with that last word, but he caught himself and gave her an appraising look.

Interesting. Maëline was used to people telling her their life stories moments after they'd met her. She had the kind of face that made them feel at ease to share things they wouldn't ordinarily. The interesting bit here was that he'd stopped himself. Now, for the first time in her life, she wondered if she could get him to continue.

'Yes,' she said softly. 'It's a big house to fill by yourself.'

'Hm,' was his only answer.

'What was he like, your uncle?'

David raised his eyebrows and blinked. In Maëline's head, the jump from living alone in a big house to wanting to know about the previous person who'd done so wasn't very big. She was curious to find out which of the rooms had belonged to him. Perhaps she could match the vibes to the person. But David must have had very different thoughts because her question surprised him.

'Oh! Err... He was... nice. Old-fashioned. Straightforward. Things were a certain way with him, and woe to those who tried to change his mind.' He snorted. 'But he loved having all the family together in this house. He always made sure there were plenty of sweets for Julie and me. I think…' Again, he cast Maëline an appraising look, but this time he continued. 'I think he would have loved to have children of his own, but his wife died very young, and I believe he never got over it. If you look in the room above this one, there are pictures of his wife all over the walls and on every surface.'

The sad, cold room. That made sense. But now Maëline was even more curious about the room in the back. As long as he was talking, maybe she could get him to explain without seeming like 'the weirdo who felt evil in a room'. She guessed David was not the type to appreciate those sorts of sensations.

'So what made you choose the back room? Of all the rooms upstairs, it has the least amount of sunshine.'

He shrugged. 'It's closest to the stairs and has an en-suite. Easy.'

'Hm.' She nodded, more because she didn't know how else to dig for more information than that she agreed with his reasoning.

'I mean, they'd already got rid of the swastikas, so…' He grinned apologetically, obviously enjoying the shock she knew would be written on her face. 'They're still there in the basement, but since I hardly ever use that, I'll deal with them later.'

'But... What...' Maëline had some trouble picking the right question out of all the ones pushing to the front of her mind.

'My great-grandfather. Among family we say that he didn't know what he was doing, but we all know he was a bad man. My bedroom used to be his study, a place he'd... decorated extensively. But that was all so long ago. For me, that room is just the most convenient.'

'You don't think it's kept, *alors*... some of its ghosts?'

He threw his head back and laughed. 'Oh no, the ghosts are older.'

Maëline's eyes widened.

'You don't believe in ghosts, do you?' He seemed quite amused at the thought.

'Well, no, not precisely that.' *But you never know, do you?*

'Good. Otherwise you'd have come to the wrong part of the Beaujolais. Plenty of stories around here. But I prefer to look towards the future instead of the past.'

'Oh? You have plans for this house?' A politely curious smile played around her lips.

He glanced around the room. 'Like I said, can't get rid of it. But maybe, if I can update it, I can rent it out. Needs a lot of work, though. Better central heating, insulation, better Wi-Fi...'

'Gaming room?' She pointed her chin towards the cabinet with the TV.

He shrugged. 'It's something to do, *quoi*.'

'I bet I can slaughter you at *Mario Kart*.'

Both his eyebrows shot up, and a slow grin spread across his face. 'I'll take that bet.'

He obviously had no idea how many hours of experience she had. Giddy at the prospect of applying her usual, inoffensive, gentle way to put him firmly in his place, she darted off the couch to close the shutters behind the TV, so they could see what they were doing.

When she opened the window, a light at the bottom of the garden caught her eye. But as soon as she focussed her attention on it, it was gone.

David must have noticed her hesitation because he asked if something was wrong.

'No... Only... You know those abandoned buildings down there? Do they belong to you?'

He nodded, questions in his eyes.

'They're empty?'

Another nod.

'Julie went over there when she came because she'd seen something move. And just now, I thought I saw a light on.' Biting her lip, she stared at the sad structure, alone in the snow, where all was quiet and dark once more. She closed the shutters and the window, and smiled at David. 'You know what, I think it's Julie's suggestion playing tricks on me. It could have just been a reflection on the window when I opened it.'

'But there's no sun.'

She shrugged. 'Let's just play. It's probably nothing.'

'We'll check it out later.' He took the controller she handed him and made space for her on the couch beside him, putting his leg up on the coffee table.

The next hour they spent laughing and trying to outdo one another, though Maëline felt it prudent to let him win every now and then. Staying in his good graces seemed to be easier than she'd thought at first, but it was still essential. When it was time to start making lunch, she tried to let him win one more time, but he was absolute rubbish. There was no way she could let him win without it being obvious.

'You're a cheat! You let me win!' She exclaimed when the animals on screen were doing their victory lap.

He threw down his controller and put his hands up in defence. 'Not true. I picked the wrong car, that's all.'

'On purpose.' She narrowed her eyes at him, making him laugh.

'*Je te jure*, you won fair and square.'

She gave up and leaned back on the couch.

'This is much more fun together,' he mused.

'Isn't it?' Her enthusiasm was out before she knew it. And David noticed. Oh no, now he would ask about her life, and she'd have to either clam up or lie, neither of which would help her stay here.

He was silent for a beat before he spoke. 'I thought you'd have loads of friends.'

Ha! Not the remark she'd expected, but also not one she could give an honest reply to. 'Why would you say that?'

He hesitated again, then looked her in the eye. 'You're... sweet. And fun. Cute.'

Heat flushed her cheeks. Now that was the perfect lead-up to a kiss. Was he going to kiss her? He wasn't supposed to. He was her client. But would she mind? She inadvertently held her breath.

His phone rang. His only reaction at first was a slight tightening of his lips, but then he reached for his mobile.

'It's only my friend Manu.'

'Take it,' she blurted before he'd finished speaking. She let out her breath and jumped off the couch. 'Drink? No? I'll just... take these to the kitchen.' She hid her face while collecting their coffee cups from earlier. She couldn't be sure kissing had been on his mind, but it had been on hers and that was very, very inconvenient. Time to flee to the kitchen and cool off. Peeling potatoes was just the thing.

After about four potatoes, David hobbled in. 'Maëline? My friend Manu is coming over. I hope you don't mind. He more or less invited himself.'

She shook her brown curls. 'Why should I mind?'

Looking not quite directly at her, he shrugged. 'You're here now. I don't want him to bother you.'

It was almost funny how much he was not used to having someone else around. 'I'm here to make your life easier, not more complicated. You can do whatever you want, and I'll work around it.'

'Good. Good, that's what I want.' He nodded for emphasis. Whatever he did want, it wasn't that. 'So anyway, he owns the Château de Montmales...'

That made Maëline look up from her potatoes.

Still avoiding her gaze, David scuffed his crutches on the floor. 'But he's one of my oldest friends. He's not into that whole vicomte thing. He says he's the same person with or without the title of viscount.'

'Okay.' Maëline nodded slowly, not sure why this introduction made him so uncomfortable. Did he think she'd act like a starstruck groupie? Had that happened before?

'*D'accord*... Okay. He'll be here after lunch. I told him we were going to check the buildings for trapped animals, and he said not to because he wanted to come over.' David gave a nervous chuckle. 'He can get a bit authoritarian like that, but he's really a good guy. You'll see.'

'Okay,' Maëline said again, not sure what he expected of her.

He readied his crutches to go back to the sitting room, but didn't seem comforted at all.

'Would you like me to make tea when he gets here?' What else could she say?

He paused, looking perplexed at first, but then broke into a slow smile. 'No, he only ever drinks sparkling water and wine. He'll get his own. But thank you for offering.'

Whether it had been the right thing to say or not, David's shoulders seemed to relax a little, so she went with it. 'Does he live alone in his castle too?'

'No, he has even more ghosts than I do.'

It was meant to be a joke, but it reminded Maëline of the cold sadness she'd felt upstairs and she shivered.

'Actually, he lives there with his mother. She hasn't set foot outside those walls since his dad died. Such a shame. She's one lovely lady, the vicomtesse.' He hopped towards the kitchen counter and leaned against it. 'You know...'

Maëline looked up, as his tone meant a change of subject.

He held her gaze and said softly, 'I'm not at all sorry any more that I've had to cut my holiday short.'

She stared at him for a long second, then asked, 'Do you want broccoli or green beans for lunch?'

Coward.

5

Get rid of him, now!

Beau and I trudged through the snow that was beginning to pile up along the road to the village. I should probably have worn boots without heels, but what is a strong boy for if not to lean on when you've made a little wardrobe mistake. I couldn't contain my excitement about Maile's new venture and babbled on about it, when he suddenly yanked me back. I yelped. A white van whooshed past, inches from my toes.

'Are you okay?' Poor Thibault looked more shocked than I felt at first. But when the wave of surprise and fear and anger hit, it rolled right out of my mouth in the form of the foulest words I could think of. Beau seemed more shocked by my language than by the close call. He stared at me, eyes big as saucers, but then couldn't stop laughing until we reached the café, which annoyed me even more.

All throughout the meal, he kept wondering whether the food would taste good in such a foul mouth. He even repeated my stream of filth almost word for word to my friend Jeanette

Ta, who owned the café. She clapped her hands over her ears in mock horror, but the two of them together soon got me over my anger. Despite this being my second almost-accident of the day, I had to laugh along.

'Where did you even learn such words? I might tell your mother.' Jeanette crossed her arms over her apron, looking down on me.

'I have an app. Learn a new word every day, dirty version.'

'I might need that one. I have a meeting with the architect on Friday.' She cast her gaze skywards. Fixing up the old hotel just off the village square had been her lifelong dream. Now that I made more money than I knew what to do with, I had invested in her dream, but there was still a long way to go until it would become a reality. With a sigh, she brought us our food, and I squeezed her arm by way of encouragement when she left the table to wait on the people next to us. Too late I realised one of them was Bella Dudevant, one of my least favourite people in the village.

'Juliiie! Have you met Marcel Carlier?' Bella indicated her companion. He was a rather nondescript man in his fifties, his most interesting feature being a greying little moustache. He wore dark greyish-green tweed, and though I couldn't see his legs under the table, I half expected knickerbockers. Knowing Bella, his redeeming qualities were probably measured in currencies, which would explain the arrogance oozing from his eyes.

Marcel acknowledged me with a nod. 'Madame.'

'Marcel knows everyone who's anyone in the Beaujolais. Don't you, *loulou*?' I was glad that didn't include me, though technically he did now know me. Did that mean I had been promoted? 'He's going up to the château, naturally, and I'm still trying to make him let me come.' She pouted in what I assumed was her seductive way.

Jeanette interrupted to take their orders, which I took as my chance to get out of further conversation by turning my back on them. As much as I longed to be part of the village again, some of its inhabitants I could do without. I tried not to pay any more attention to them, but when Beau started an animated monologue on vintage motorcycles, I couldn't help but overhear some of our neighbours' talk.

The gravelly voice of a man who'd smoked too much for too long said, 'Let's just eat. I'm not used to these small village eateries.'

Bella's crooning voice answered, 'So will you take me to Bocuse's next time?'

'We'll see. I hate the fact that everyone knows me there, but at least I won't have to put up with this' – his cutlery scraped across the plate – 'whatever it is.'

How dare he! People came from miles around to taste Théo's delicious traditional meals. He'd won prizes in the Lyonese *bouchon* where he used to work. He was one of the reasons why investing in Jeanette's dream had not been such a risk for me.

Bella tinkled a laugh. 'I hate the sound of the first glass of wine being poured from a bottle. Doesn't stop me drinking it, though!'

Thibault's phone waving under my nose, showing a picture of some motorcycle, brought me back to my own company. Soon, our food arrived and I forgot all about the little tweedy toad.

After lunch, I felt a little rosy, having had an extra glass of wine. Normally I don't indulge, but I had two weeks off starting now, so why not celebrate with some local goodness?

'Since I have nothing better for you to do, would you mind getting some groceries for me?' I asked Thibault.

He yawned. 'Sure, text me a list. Need anything from the baker?'

'Can't live without a fresh baguette. But you can get one from the supermarket.'

'*Pas de soucis*, the ones from the baker are so much better.'

I grinned. Beau would always make an excuse to visit the bakery. Céline, the baker's daughter, was a lifelong friend, and the person who usually delivered cupcakes at the end of each of my sessions. Having been robbed of her delightful company today, it was no wonder he didn't mind getting me some bread.

We paid and left, drawing our coats close to weather the cold on the short walk home. As we passed the wrought-iron gates to La Grande Maison, I wondered how my brother was doing. Should I pay him another visit, or would that be considered butting in? I decided against it for now. Maybe I'd drop in later today with a little *goûter*, an afternoon snack usually reserved for children, but one that I knew both David and I had kept going when we grew up. A piece of chocolate cake, for instance. Or caramel. David liked caramel. Always had had a sweet tooth.

We rounded a white van parked on the pavement. Was it the same one that had almost killed me earlier? All white vans look the same to me. The fact that it was parked in front of the empty buildings on David's estate was a bit odd, though. Built in the region's iconic yellow stone, these dilapidated structures had been abandoned as far as I could remember. If the van was there for the buildings, then maybe David had decided to finally do something about that eyesore. It would also explain the movement I saw earlier. Perhaps he'd turn them into businesses? They seemed a bit small for residences.

Once back in my cosy, toasty kitchen, I stripped off all the excess layers and gathered the ingredients for a caramel cake. Should be just about ready by four, right in time to bring my brother a *goûter*. While Beau grabbed a shopping bag and headed out again, I video-called my best friend.

'I wish he'd make a decision that wasn't exactly what I would want him to do but would never ask him to!' I wailed by way of a greeting. I hadn't intended to start with negativity. In fact, I'd already forgotten I'd been annoyed with Beau before. But as soon as I saw Tiana, it just came out.

'And hello to you too,' was Tiana's answer. 'Yes, that sounds very logical. A man who does exactly what you want him to without asking. Get rid of him, now!' Tiana pulled up an eyebrow and skewered me with her striking jade gaze.

'I'd hardly call him a man,' I muttered. Well, what else could I say? I know I was being childish and unreasonable, but it was my house, and there he... *was*.

The only man I'd had in here before was the stray cat I'd named Henri. But Henri didn't walk around as if he owned the place. In fact, he didn't even want to come in. Whenever he'd come to me for cuddles and I'd taken him inside, he'd escaped at the first opportunity. Now he more or less lived in my garden. Whenever he felt like it. Still, that was different. You know, because he's a cat.

I leaned the phone against a jar of pasta on the counter and started weighing my ingredients for the caramel cake. 'I mean, he *told* me to go and see you while he did the groceries. Of course I *want* to see you, but I don't want him to *tell* me.'

Tiana tapped her lip. 'Maybe you should go away somewhere. Check into a hotel, go skiing, or catch some rays on Réunion. Leave the man to do what you want him to do without you seeing him.'

I simpered some more. 'But it's my house. He should be the one to leave.'

'Then tell him to get his own place.'

'I can't just kick him out!'

Throwing both hands in the air, Tiana produced a frustrated sound that was very unladylike. 'Look, Julie, if you don't want to get rid of him, you're going to have to learn to live with him. So stop whining about it.'

'So you think I should go on holiday.' Her narrowed eyes didn't deter me from ignoring her sage advice. I'd measured my dry ingredients and got the butter out. 'I think I'd prefer the Caribbean to Réunion. Want to come?'

'*Non.* I'm on a deadline. But I do have a new book for you if you are going.'

I wasn't. 'I'll always read your books.' She wrote romances and I read them. What better combination? She didn't need to know I wouldn't be reading it on a beach. I didn't like travel much. Though I was beginning to make a bit of a name for myself, I'd already turned down one or two speaking opportunities at conferences because they were halfway across the planet. Maybe it would add to my allure if I was an eccentric artist who never left my village.

'Since you're not going anywhere,' Tiana continued, 'would you like to join Lucas and me for the Nouveau concert in Villefranche on Thursday? I'm sure I can get an extra ticket.'

I gave her a sweet smile. 'Thanks, Ti, that sounds lovely. It'll be good to get out.' I had to give her that. 'Is it outdoors, though? They say the snow's going to get thick over the next few days.'

'It's in the *salle des fêtes*, so we'll be fine. Can you believe snow this early in November? I'm sure it'll all be melted by Thursday.'

Looking out the window at the tiny flecks of white fluttering by, I put down my spoon. 'Let's hope so. Look, I'm going to turn my mixer on, so I'll talk to you later.'

We said our goodbyes and I started creaming my butter and sugar together. While I worked, I considered my own outburst. Thibault wasn't a bad house guest. Not at all. But he was always there, even if it was across the courtyard. And when people came over, there he was. When I visited others, there he was again. People, including Beau sometimes, had started to see us as a unit, and I was *not* happy with that. I sighed. Maybe I should follow Tiana's advice and get out of here for a while.

With a lovely caramel cake decorated with sugared hazelnuts in my cake box, I wrapped myself in every warm thing I could find to trek through the cold to my brother's villa. Beau had not yet returned from his shopping trip, so I had a feeling I knew where to find him. The *boulangerie* was only about fifty yards down the street from La Grande Maison anyway, so while I was dressed for an Arctic expedition, I might as well get my step count up.

The bell above the door tinkled and who should I see but the ever-present Thibault, lurking in a corner.

'You're still here?'

His blond mop turned towards me, an airy smile lingering on his lips. 'Don't act so surprised. I said I'd get the groceries. I have everything for a *filet de porc en cocotte* with fennel and cider, but I've bought a nice fresh sea bass. Thought we could have that tomorrow and we can keep the pork for the day after. That way we won't have to brave the snow for a few days.'

Madame Dufaux, the only other person in the shop, performed an open-mouthed stare, not unlike the sea bass Beau had mentioned. She recovered with a shake of her frizzy curls. 'Sounds divine. My husband cooks, but he never cleans up after himself. Still, could be worse.' She shrugged, paid, and marched home to a husband we all knew she adored.

Céline winked at me. 'Better make sure you do those dishes too, Thibault. Or you might end up in the "Could be worse" pile.'

'I'll have you know, I'm the bee's knees of men.' He struck a pose, showing off all his assets, but neither Céline nor I were impressed.

Céline leaned over the glass counter. 'Tiny and bent?'

I choked and spluttered at the same time, then burst out laughing.

Clutching his heart, Beau sank to his knees. '*Et tu, Brute?* I thought you were my friend!'

Céline only grinned, but I was wiping tears from my eyes. A moment before, I'd been annoyed with him for again assuming I would be there to have lunch together tomorrow, but with the laughter at his expense, my irritation washed away. It wasn't all his fault that I didn't seem to have a moment without him some days. We had worked a lot, and since he was learning from me as well, we'd spent even more time together. I guessed I did need that break after all. Now where could I go?

Peering up at me from down on his knees, Thibault asked, 'So why are *you* here?'

'I'm taking this cake to David and thought you might like to join me for a piece.' I eyed the almond croissants. No, I didn't really have an excuse for those extra calories. But if I swapped it for a piece of my own cake...

Beau got up from the floor, his eyes on Céline, but she wasn't going to answer for him. She'd seen my greedy glance.

'Go on.' Céline knew my weakness all too well. 'Who would know?'

I patted my hips. 'They add up, you know.'

'Isn't that why you wear a petticoat?' Thibault dared to ask.

I stuck my nose in the air and took one of the alluring pastries off the stack. 'So maybe my moon is a little fuller than everybody else's. We can't all be *croissants*.'

Bite. Taste. Melt. My eyes rolled back in pure delight. These were the best. Two sets of amused eyes were watching me when I opened mine again. I shrugged. Who wants to be a crescent moon when there's almond croissants around? 'I'm proud of my be-ooty.'

Thibault groaned. 'Juju, that doesn't work. I know you're desperate to use it, but let it die in peace, please?' He turned to Céline. 'I actually came for a *flûte*. Might as well add the croissant to the bill.'

Miffed that my play on words wasn't appreciated, I snapped, 'You're not fooling anyone, paying with my money.'

Ignoring me, Thibault lifted his grocery bag. 'I have everything else. Want to hear Isabelle's latest wisdom?'

I looked up. The butcher's wife was usually good for an unconventional remark or two. Though I preferred the country sayings that André, the village gardener and street cleaner, spouted every so often, Isabelle was comically convinced of the truth in her own words.

Thibault assumed a tone eerily close to that of Isabelle. 'If you're so old that you're braking for a truck coming the other way, you should have a warning sign on your car.' In his own voice, he continued, 'I don't even know why she said it. I walked in on that jewel. Anyway, I'll follow you and your cake. See you later, Céline.'

'Have you ever considered acting?' I asked him while we braved the cold and the ever-thickening snow.

He wrinkled his nose. 'Nah, I'd get stage fright. Doing the same thing over and over every night would be the death of me.'

Speaking of death... The near-fatal white van was still there. Good, that gave me a topic of conversation: did David *want* his sister dead?

6

I have an invitation for you all

Maëline got up from her renewed search for out-of-date food cans to answer the doorbell.

'Who is it?' David called from the living room.

'Cake,' she answered. Cake with a petticoat. The cake lowered to reveal the sister. 'Love your skirt.' From under the mountain of cold-repellent clothing peeped a bit of fabric covered in pictures of cat faces.

'Oh, thank you,' Julie cooed. 'I love your style too, but I can't pull off tight knitwear. I need a bit of floof to hide the rolls.' She marched past Maëline, slamming the door shut behind her. 'That snow is ridiculous. I might have to camp out here if it continues like that. Thibault's on his way, but there was so much snow already that the gate wouldn't close. I told him to leave it, but he wanted to be manly or something.' Shoving the cake in Maëline's hands, she pulled off a thick wool coat, a long chunky scarf, and two giant mittens. 'It's cold,' she added superfluously.

'No hat?'

Julie shuddered. 'Those are extreme measures. You can never get your hair quite right after you wear them.' With a flick of her ponytail, she sailed into the living room.

In a way, brother and sister were very much alike, though they clearly didn't think so. Acting like you own the place is logical when you actually own the place, but there was a little too much confidence in both of them. But they were nice enough, if a little grumpy at first in David's case.

On her way to the kitchen, Maëline could hear the siblings bicker. Something about a lethal van. Were they always like that? Their poor parents. She sliced four pieces of cake and returned to the sitting room.

'What a lovely thought to bring your brother cake.' She knew the impact of her soft voice all too well.

David's mouth closed mid-word, and Julie looked decidedly smug.

'Living so close, you must help each other out all the time. That's so nice.' Gone was the smugness. These two were like children together.

In the silence that followed, the doorbell rang again. A tall, rather lanky young man with a flaxen moustache smiled broadly at her when she opened the door. His hair was hidden under a silly wool hat with ear flaps and a large pompom on top. The thing was pink and purple, sporting a pattern of unicorns, and did not go with his stylish coat at all. Maëline liked him instantly.

'You must be Maëline. I'm Manu.'

Smiling back, Maëline stepped aside to let him in. When he passed her, she noticed one of his eyes was brown, the other icy blue. But instead of being disconcerting, it made him look exotic and alluring. Maëline's mind conjured up images of him in a top hat, cape, and monocle. He'd look absolutely smashing. She wondered if he could do magic tricks. If not, he should.

Manu had gone in ahead of her. 'Excellent! I could do with something sweet. Oh, caramel. Someone knows you too well, *mec.*'

Again, the doorbell rang. This time it was the pushy assistant, or the answer to all women's prayers, as he seemed to view himself.

'Bonsoir, mon oisillon.' What was his problem? Did he call everyone his little bird, or was this a special treatment for her? He actually winked at her!

Maëline stuck her head out to see if there was anyone else coming, but Thibault seemed to be the last one. Introductions were being made in the sitting room, but Maëline was quite happy to escape the company just a little longer while she sliced another piece of cake. Though the people she helped through her work varied quite a lot in background, this was on another level of different. These people owned a mansion, a château, and an internationally thriving photography business. And here she was without even an official roof over her head. She decided to make a pot of tea, just to keep her away a little longer.

When she finally entered the living room again, the hubbub had died down to civil conversation. It took Maëline a while to realise they were talking about art. Most of the names dropped she'd never heard of, but apparently Manu was planning to either buy, sell, or display a valuable painting.

'More tea, anyone?' she asked in a moment's quiet. She wasn't contributing anyway. Might as well keep everyone hydrated. But she hadn't been in the kitchen a minute when Julie joined her.

'I don't care about old paintings either,' she confessed. 'Can I give you a hand?'

'Not much to do. But I'd love some company.'

Julie set herself down on one of the kitchen chairs. 'Fine art's great and all, but I prefer good entertainment. Like this.' She pulled her business card out of a hidden pocket in the folds of her skirt. One side held her business information, the other showed a picture of her with an iris, sticking her tongue out the way the flower does. She'd obviously used a mirror to take the picture, since the camera showed as well. Julie sighed. 'It's no good, since it doesn't really display the kind of work

I do at all, but I hand them out to people who might want something different. I suppose it's art in a way, but for me, the entertainment value is more important. Buy a Vermeer, you get a pretty picture and a bunch of status. Buy one of my photos, you get a pretty picture and a fun memory. Now which is more valuable in the end?'

Was that a trick question?

Luckily, Julie didn't require an answer. 'Are you going to be okay in this big house? If you need any help, I'm just a short walk away.'

'I'll be fine, thanks.' This was her job. If Julie was so eager to help, why had she engaged Maëline in the first place? But then David's face popped into her head. Hm, yeah, okay. Not the easiest person to try and help. She'd caught him several times already, attempting to get down to the cellar on the world's narrowest steps, or balancing on one foot to pick up something he'd dropped. After her first reprimand, the thunderstorm had brewed above his head, but again her soft voice had saved her, and he seemed to have accepted that she was here to do those things for him in the coming weeks.

'David's already said not to bother with the rest of the house.'

Julie snorted. 'Of course not. I don't know why he's so adamant to keep it on and even to live in it. I'd have sold it to a developer years ago, but apparently, it's our heritage and we can't touch it. He told you what happened, didn't he?'

Maëline shook her head.

'My grandfather was the middle of three children, and the only one who'd produced any offspring. His elder brother had lived and died in this mansion, while his younger sister was the previous owner of my house. When my grandfather died, the house came to my dad, who didn't know what to do with it, so it was empty for years. People in the village even started to make up stories about it being haunted. After dad died, my mother had it appraised, but because of the stories, we couldn't have sold it for a good price even if we'd wanted to. So when David got this job, he moved in here. The ghosts weren't real, and if they were, they were family. That was his view, anyway.'

Did ghosts mind if you were family? Maëline sure wasn't. But she didn't believe in ghosts, did she?

Julie had already found something else to babble about, but Maëline was left with the memory of that light she'd seen in the empty buildings. Did ghosts make lights?

'We should probably get back in there, before the tea gets cold,' Julie pointed out.

Right. Focus on the practical things. Tea. Tea existed. Tea was never malicious. Unless you counted green tea. Yuck.

'So I have an invitation for you all,' Manu was saying when they entered the room. 'I know it's last-minute, but I'd like you all to come to the château tomorrow and stay for the Beaujolais Nouveau celebrations.'

Everyone stayed silent. Julie narrowed her eyes, Thibault broke into a grin, and David— Why was David staring at her?

He was the first to speak. 'You don't mean me, right? I'm broken.'

'Of course I mean you! I'm in *your* house, I'm *your* friend, who else would I mean? And you'll have Maëline to help you, and now Julie and Thibault as well, if they want.'

'They want,' Beau said. 'Don't they?'

Oh, that's why Julie kept him around! The pleading puppy-dog eyes. Maëline thought she'd be able to deal with them, but Julie was not made of stern enough stuff.

'Sure, why not.' She didn't look too happy about it, though.

David shook his head. 'I don't want to spring a change of location on Maëline. She didn't sign up for that.'

'For an exclusive party with a lot of free wine? Or don't they allow you to drink?' Manu directed this at Maëline.

'I don't mind. I don't drink anyway.'

'There! Come on, Dav, you love this stuff. You were the one sulking that I didn't invite you in the first place, even though you were supposed to be on holiday. I thought you'd jump at this. I mean, I have a magician coming and everything.'

For some reason that made David snort. Must be an in-joke.

'Maëline, say you'll come. Then he'll have to.' He marched over to her and put his arm around her shoulders, making sad, pleading faces at his friend, who showed all the signs of gathering his thundercloud again.

She smiled. 'That's not really how it works. I go where he goes.'

'But you want to come, *non*? Unless you'd rather go fox-hunting in some abandoned shack.' In her head, there was a cape dangling off his outstretched arm. She'd love to see him in his natural habitat. But David didn't seem too eager and he shouldn't have to go because of her, so she shrugged.

'Of course she does.' Manu had already turned back to David. 'Come on!'

His eyes on Maëline, David sighed. 'All right.'

Throwing his hands in the air, Manu laughed. 'Man! I never expected to have to convince you to come to the event of the year. It's going to be so much fun – you'll see. It's only a couple of days anyway. I'm kicking you back down the mountain on Friday.'

David huffed. 'So who else is coming?'

'Oh, you know.' Manu waved the question away. 'The schmoozers, the boozers, and the bobos. All the guys are still on holiday.'

Though Manu continued the conversation with Thibault, David's face fell. He'd told her he wasn't disappointed about the holiday any more, but part of him must consider the party small compensation for the abandoned trip.

Julie and Beau didn't stay long after that, and when they left, Julie hugged David, who tried to duck out of the embrace. One of these days, Maëline would find out why he could not be an adult around his sister. Manu left as well, and Maëline got a tray from the kitchen to clear away the cups and plates.

'Are you sure you don't mind going?' David now asked her.

'Of course not. Could be fun. At the very least it'll keep you from going stir crazy in the house. That's what gets to most active people in a situation like this.'

'Hm.' He was silent for a beat, then almost hesitatingly asked, 'So what did you think of Manu?'

'He's great. I don't know why you seem to think I wouldn't like him. He's charming. Love his hat.'

He gave a reluctant smile. 'Yeah, he's crazy. Well, not crazy. A strong personality, I think you'd call it. He usually gets what he wants. Good thing, too, in his case.'

'You mean because he owns a castle? Hang on, I'll be right back.' She brought the dirty dishes to the kitchen and stacked them in the dishwasher. By the time she was done, he'd followed her into the kitchen.

'Did you notice a difference in Beau's behaviour?'

'Not really, but I've only seen him once before.'

'Mm, yes...' Seemingly deep in thought, he leaned heavily on his crutches. 'Never thought I might actually like him. Very strange.' He shook himself out of it. 'Anyway, back to Manu. There are a few things you should probably know before we go. Manu inherited the title and the estate at the age of twenty-one, when his father died. He's been running it ever since, pretty much on his own, because his mother never got over the old vicomte's death. Like I said, she hasn't left the château since. There was a time no one was even allowed to enter, but that changed in a big way when Manu opened the place up as a venue for weddings and such. She usually stays out of the limelight, but I'm sure you'll get to meet her in the coming days. She's lovely, but in case she seems a bit out of touch, now you know why.'

It had come out as a continuous stream. Maëline blinked a few times. 'Okay. Thanks.' Apparently, it was important that she knew this right now, but the relevance of it escaped her. David, however, seemed relieved to get it off his chest, so she smiled reassuringly.

'So... you like him?'

She nodded.

'You don't think he's a bit... arrogant?'

'Not that I've seen.'

'He can be a real pain.'

Maëline narrowed her eyes. Wasn't Manu supposed to be his friend?

'But you like him?'

'Yes?' She did, but now she wasn't sure she wouldn't be kicked out if she said so.

'Hm.' He returned to the sitting room, and she continued her inventory of the kitchen. Whatever his reasons were, she'd probably find out tomorrow.

7

Coffee in the petit salon

'What was that all about?' In the light of a street lamp, I stared at this new Thibault I didn't know at all.

'What, the posh voice and the la-di-da?'

'Uh-huh.' I couldn't even form real words any more. He'd blended in with the other men as if he'd known them all his life.

'Oh, it's just a trick. Imitate people's manners so they think you fit in. This one was just funny. He's such a bobo.'

'And you're such a beau, Beau.' He was right, though. Technically, of course, *bourgeois bohème* didn't apply to Hugues-Emmanuel Blanc-Mattieu, Vicomte de Montmales, because he was literally entitled, but all the behaviour fit. 'Did you fake the stuff about old masters too?'

He laughed. 'No, that was just coincidence. I used to copy a lot of that stuff in my drawings. Still do, sometimes. If they'd been talking about stocks, they'd have found me out in a matter of seconds. Well, maybe minutes. I am quite good at this.'

'Pffft!' Humility was an empty entry in Beau's dictionary. But though he usually meant these things, he joked about them, too, so I laughed along as I opened my front door and stamped the snow off my boots. 'Better get packing, I suppose.'

He beamed at that. 'Yeah! That was a bit of luck, wasn't it? Your client yesterday said it was the place to be, and now we get to be there.'

'Yay, lucky us.' I tried not to sound too sarcastic, but Beau shoved my shoulder.

'You're such a granny. For someone in such a social profession, you're remarkably antisocial.'

'I'm not! I prefer to be social in a smaller group, that's all.'

'And on your own turf, where everyone does what you say, I presume?'

'That would be the most desirable circumstance, yes.'

He tutted. Yes, he actually tutted me.

'May I remind you that you are in fact on my turf right now and you should do as I tell you?'

He grinned. 'You wish. Only when we're working. It's in my contract.'

'It is not.'

'It is. I pencilled it in after you signed it.'

'Go!' I put two hands on his back and shoved him out the courtyard door. I heard him laugh all the way to the studio. Idiot. I grinned too.

Beau startled me when he came into the kitchen the next morning, his hair a mess and his eyes in grumpy mode.

'You do have your own kitchen in there.'

'It's not a kitchen, it's a cupboard,' he mumbled. 'It does have coffee, but then I couldn't scare you.'

Hm. Beau-grin before coffee was more like Beau-grimace. Scary wasn't the right word exactly, but he wasn't far off. He still moaned about the shiny fake kitchen in my studio being bigger than the real one in his part of it. Not that he ever used it. Apart from the coffee maker, that is. Usually, by the time he entered my kitchen for more coffee, he'd already had some in his and made sure he looked presentable. So what was different today?

'To what do I owe the honour of your glorious presence this morning?'

His only answer was a grunt, while he poured himself a cup.

'Want me to order you a cupcake?'

Now he truly glared at me.

The wise thing to do would be to leave him be, but instead I reached out and nudged his cup towards his lips. 'There's a good boy. Drink this, it'll make you feel better.'

He took a sip, then chuckled. 'You are so annoying.'

'*Merci bien.*'

'That enormous thing yours?' He hitched his thumb over his shoulder, pointing at my – apparently sizeable? – suitcase. I mean, I would say it was perfect for a few days away, but I do need a few more items than an ordinary person. Wouldn't want to look like an ordinary person, would I? Branding, that's what it was. I was packed and ready to go, and that was the important thing here.

I'd already checked the cat-flap was working. Henri was nowhere to be seen, but he knew he could come in and find food and shelter here. I hoped he'd be all right while I was gone. I hoped *I* would be. I'd become quite attached to my little stray.

I typed a text to Tiana. *Going away for a few days.*

Her answer came back immediately. *Yay!*

Me: *Beau's coming.*

Tiana: *Oh. Well, enjoy anyway!*

Me: *Would you mind checking in on Henri for me?*

Tiana: *NP TTYL*

No problem. Talk to you later. Maybe I was weird, but I couldn't see the abbreviations without saying the full words in my head, even with the familiar LOL. Laughing out loud. Stop it!

There was only one thing I still needed before we left. The new memory card for my camera. Where had I left it? I went through every place in the house I could think of and searched my entire studio, but that stupid little card eluded me. Maybe it was upstairs? Beau had gone out to the bakery for breakfast, so I could nip upstairs and have a quick peek. Since he'd moved in, I had hardly set foot in what was now his domain, so the chances of finding my card there were pretty slim, but you never know, right?

I scaled the stairs and took in my surroundings, but none of my aunt's old furniture showed signs of containing my card. Since there wasn't much more than a bed, a desk, a couch, an armchair, and one chest of drawers, that wasn't very strange. I didn't want to go through Thibault's things, but couldn't resist opening the desk drawer, the one place where my memory card might hide. It didn't.

But what I did find, to my surprise, was the empty frame that had once held one of the keys from my collection. What would Beau want with my framed key? There was a question with a thousand answers right in front of me. The desk was littered with Beau's drawings, and more spilled out of a sketchbook that had been underneath the frame in the drawer.

Still, why would he take a frame off my wall when I paid him more than enough to buy one for himself? Even if he liked the style, or whatever other reason he could have had for choosing this one, he might have asked me for it. I grumbled some more about backgrounds and upbringing and hearty words when he got back, but I really had to find that memory card now.

I eventually found it slipped under my keyboard just as Thibault returned from the bakery. By then I'd forgotten all about the frame. We had a quick breakfast, threw our bags in the car, and headed off. Snow had fallen through the night and continued to fall in large, soft puffs. Beau had put his muscles to good work before going to the bakery and cleared a path from my car to the road. The roads had been cleared earlier, but on the less-used streets such as the one leading to my *quartier*, the white blanket was already piling up again.

The same was true for the road leading up to the Château de Montmales. Up to the outer gates everything was fine, but on the castle grounds the normally bumpy gravel road had now become slippery as well. Thibault found my little screams and frightened whoops hilarious, but I caught him uttering one himself after we'd switched seats.

I was quite happy when we'd parked the car and now only had to cross the old drawbridge. The château de Montmales was built on a rocky outcrop of the mountain, connected only by a bridge. Though the snow made the surface tricky to navigate, the bridge was wide enough not to be scary. They'd also had to put up railings for visitors, but not many were brave enough to get that close to the edge. The dip between the castle rock and the mountain proper might not run all that deep, but your chances of survival were probably quite slim if you did happen to drop off. Which is why I should probably not have worn boots with heels. Again. I clung to Beau's arm, just to be sure.

While the château de Montmales itself had exterior walls made of smooth blocks of stone, the protective wall surrounding it was rough. Here and there bits of moss and tiny weeds had found a foothold and a place to grow, but at the moment, most of the protruding stones were covered in snow. We entered the courtyard through the Gothic gate with its heavy, wrought-iron portcullis around ten o'clock. I'd expected people to be running around preparing for the festivities, but everything was peaceful inside these walls. The yellow stones of the castle were muted to a dull ecru in the grey light.

To the right, a solitary tree stood shivering in the wind, though the walls held back the full force of the growing storm. To the left was the entrance to the château – twelve steps leading to a small terrace, flanked by slender, round towers. No footprints appeared in the snow anywhere in the courtyard. Though the snow had clearly been shovelled aside earlier, that had been about two inches ago. I pulled Beau towards the castle's front door, a sturdy, oak number with a good amount of ancient nails in it and a coat of arms, complete with motto, overhead. Something about keeping it real.

'Juju! Attends!' David came slipping through the gate on three stilts. So I was Juju today, huh. That was a good omen. Maybe he'd forgiven me for butting in and sending him help. He struggled across the courtyard, but Maëline, today in an amazing cape-like coat, had apparently already learned not to offer help. Thibault, normally the first to lend a hand, never moved a muscle. When they'd reached the steps, David smiled.

'Ready to party?'

'You're keen at least.'

'Maëline didn't crash my car, so I'm happy to be here.'

Nice. I glanced at Maëline, whose only reaction was a slight tightening of the lips. David drove a classic car that he was really proud of, but this was a bit sharp, even for him. Before I could raise an eyebrow, though, the big wooden doors behind us opened.

'Welcome! David, Maëline, Julie and her young lover, you're—'

Whoa! 'No. No, he's my assistant. No love involved.' I held my hands up in defence. Manu had better get this straight right now. Before you knew it, all the guests at the party would have the wrong idea.

'Ouch, Juju.' Beau rubbed his chest. 'Not even a little?'

'Well, maybe the kind of love I'd give a naughty pet. You know, where you tell them off and then you mess up their hair.' I went to ruin the blond tsunami, but Beau dodged my hand.

Manu chuckled and bowed us into the château's hallway. Paintings, antlers, and wrought-iron light fixtures lined the walls. To my left, a giant boar's head stared at me. Across the hallway, an open gallery in dark wood ran from left to right, ending in a curved staircase. But the main attraction here was an antler-infested, wrought-iron chandelier that held both candles and electric light. Halloween must be spectacular in this place.

'Elise will see you to your rooms. Take your time to get settled. The other guests have been here since yesterday evening. *Entre nous*, boring people I've only invited because I want their money. I'm glad you're here now, so we can have some fun. We'll have a short tour of the castle at eleven, followed by coffee in the *petit salon*. At three thirty, there will be a presentation in the conference room for people interested in a partnership, but you're welcome to join.'

He left us with a slim young woman in black, who motioned us to follow her up the stairs and to the left, passing the part of the gallery that looked out both over the hallway and the dining room. It continued into a corridor that appeared surprisingly bare after the visual attack in the entrance hall, the off-white, plastered walls only broken up by dark wooden doors every so often on the right, and by leaded windows set in black frames on the left.

Elise stopped in front of one of the doors, handing a key to my brother. 'This room will be yours. If you need anything, pull the cord next to the fireplace.'

David nodded and thanked her with a smile. Thibault followed him into the room, as he'd taken the overnight bag from Maëline.

'The connecting doors are locked at the moment, but the keys are on hooks beside them. Should you want to open them, don't forget the bolts.' Elise winked at Maëline, her brown skin glowing when she looked at Beau.

The next room was Maëline's, and after that was mine. Beau's room was on the other side of some dark timber framing in the corridor, but I was too busy admiring the four-poster bed to keep an eye on my assistant. I ran my fingers over the carvings in the wood and the soft peach-coloured blankets. The blankets were obviously new, but I wondered if the bed had lived in this room for centuries, and whether anyone famous might have slept in it.

Though the window was quite small, hidden lighting around the room made it appear bright, despite the grey weather outside. I tested a small armchair in the corner and thought I would spend a lovely half hour reading my book, when there was a knock at the door.

David stumbled in when I opened it. He still had trouble with his crutches, trying to hop along without using them but falling back onto them with every second step.

'Nobody is going to think any less of you if you use those properly, you know.' I couldn't help saying it, though he'd never take advice from me and was likely to go in the opposite direction. Maybe I should stop telling him to grow up...

David threw me a look, but there weren't as many daggers in it as usual. On the contrary, he gripped his crutches more tightly and raced to the chair I had just vacated. 'She shouldn't be here.'

'You're a bit late with that.'

He sighed. 'I know. I'm sorry I yelled at you. It's actually quite... nice, you know, to have her around. To help me, I mean. But here... I don't really need her.'

I shrugged. 'So tell her that and let her enjoy the party. She has been invited, too, you know.'

'I know. But she's... I mean he... Manu, *quoi*. I...'

Where was he going with this? It wasn't like David not to have his thoughts in order. When no more words came, I tried to reassure him, although about what, I wasn't sure myself. 'Look, she's here now. You're here. You might as well enjoy it, both of you. If you don't think you need her, tell her not to bother with you. Her time's paid for anyway.'

'Hm.'

Somehow, my words had not done their job. How could they, when I had no idea what job they were supposed to be doing? 'Or not. If you think she feels she's not doing her job, invent something for her to do?' What else could it be?

'Hm.'

'David, if you don't know what you're worried about, how am I supposed to make it better?'

'You're not.' His eyes widened when he looked at me. 'Oh, is that what you thought? No, I just... Hm.'

Ah, yes, that settles that, then.

If they'd still been at his home, I might have understood. I knew exactly how annoying it could be to have someone you don't want in your house. But out here, where neither of them should have anything to do with the other if they didn't want to, that didn't really go. Also, he'd just admitted he was grateful for her help. So he both wanted her there and did not want her there. Clear as coffee dregs.

'Juju...'

Oh, he wasn't finished after all. And the rare endearment made me pay attention.

'You were always Dad's favourite—'

'What? No!' Where did that come from?

'Let me finish. You were. You're much more like him. Do you think... he chose Mum because she would fit in? Make him fit in?'

I stared at him. 'You're asking the wrong person about fitting in. Dad chose Mum because he loved her. Why would he want her to make him fit in better with his own family? And why are you suddenly questioning our parents' decision to be together?'

'You need more than love to build a relationship on. You need some sort of common ground. Like Maëline and... this castle. She shouldn't be here. They have nothing in common.'

'Maëline is marrying the castle?' My brother must have broken his head as well as his ankle. Maybe, despite his denial, he'd ordered the renovation of his outbuildings after all, meaning he was responsible for the workers nearly killing me with their white van. I narrowed my eyes at him, ready to have him committed.

He frowned, apparently irritated I did not understand his complete nonsense. 'No! I mean... Forget it.' He sank back in the chair, leaving me to wonder if we shared any genes at all.

I shrugged again, took my book out of my bag, and nestled onto the mattress. If my brother hadn't been there, I'd have moaned in utter delight! The duvet folded itself around me when I sat on it, and the pillow hugged me as if *I* were the softest thing it had ever touched. The only thing missing here was a cup of hot chocolate.

And then there was another knock. 'Julie? Have you seen David? He's not in his room, and I think we should get ready for the tour.'

Sighing, I dropped my book to the bed and heaved myself out of the pillow's embrace. 'Come on, then,' I said to David.

'I'm not going.'

'Oh? Why not?' Stupid question. His raised eyebrow confirmed that.

'Julie?' came Maëline's soft voice from the other side of the door.

'Yes, he's here. Come on in.'

Maëline opened the door but lingered on the doorstep, addressing David. 'I think we should probably get ready.'

'And I think I'm not going to put extra pressure on my ankle. I've been here before.'

I hurried towards the door and pushed Maëline out ahead of me with a hand on her shoulder. 'Let's let Mister Grumpy Pants stew, all right? I think Manu promised us coffee.'

8

So the bridge caved...

'I'm sorry, Maëline,' I said once outside the room. 'I warned you he can be pigheaded, but he's not normally this harsh. Not being able to do as he likes must have hit him hard.'

She shrugged one shoulder. 'I've dealt with frustration before. Don't worry about it. The silly thing is, he seemed fine yesterday morning. Then after Manu came round, David asked me what I thought of his friend, but the more positive things I said, the less he seemed to like it. I told him if he didn't want to go, we should excuse ourselves, but he said that wasn't it.'

I frowned, but could offer no explanation for my brother's sullen behaviour. I'd talk to him later. Right now, it was time for the castle tour, and since I'd always wanted to have a look inside, I was eager to join. David had been here countless times and told me about it, but I had never been invited before.

I knocked on Thibault's door but got no answer, so Maëline and I traced our steps back to the entrance hall. Now that

David wasn't going to slow us down, though, we were fifteen minutes early, so we took a little detour.

'Mother!'

Maëline and I looked at each other.

The door was marked *'Privé'*, but Manu's offended voice carried through to the corridor. 'You know I'd never do that. It's an heirloom. Worth much more to us than mere money.'

Whatever that meant, it wasn't intended for our ears, so we hurried along to the entrance hallway.

'I hope the tour doesn't take us outside,' Maëline said. 'Have you seen the weather? It's turned into a real storm.'

Though the hall only had a few high windows, I could see the little white tufts swirling like mad outside. If that was the case in the alcove-like entrance, around the château the gale must be going full force. I wondered if any other guests had arrived, or if they'd make it to the castle at all. I certainly wouldn't have ventured outside today if it weren't for Beau's darn puppy-dog eyes. One of these days I'd resist them.

'There's probably plenty to see inside. It's a pretty big place.' I took a step towards the double doors underneath the gallery. 'We could have a little peek. No one's here yet.'

'I'm here.'

'Sandrine! And Apolline. Corentin.' I nodded a greeting to three people I could have done without. My last client brought with her the village's most influential couple, Corentin and

Apolline Bailly. They lived in a villa halfway between my village and the château and regarded it as their seat of government. My mother was their biggest fan. I had suspected Apolline of murder not too long ago, more because I couldn't stand the way she looked down on what she called my 'little business' than anything else. Fortunately, she didn't know that.

Apolline, a thin, tall woman, gave me a patronising smile. I'd risen in her estimation after she found out how much money I made, but the way in which I earned it would always keep me on a lower tier. Her husband, a man of about my height with thinning hair and an eternal expression of boredom, looked around the hall, taking in the dead animals with a wrinkled nose. He had a habit of tilting his head backwards slightly to hide his bald patch, making him look like he wanted to look down on even people that were taller than him. I'd seen him at the council meetings my mother made me go to, but he was always distracted throughout, leaving Apolline to deal with village matters.

'Have you seen anyone else?' Sandrine asked. 'I wonder who's here.'

'Most guests won't arrive until tomorrow,' Apolline said. 'They're only invited for the day.'

'Exactly. I meant, who's here that counts.'

That wouldn't be me, then. Maëline and I exchanged a look.

'Ah, Corentin, good to see you,' said a nasal voice. A nervous-looking man with a sharp nose came in and shook Corentin's hand, ignoring everyone else. 'What a day, *hein*? What a day.'

Corentin acknowledged him with a nod. 'Gümüs.'

The lack of civility put him firmly in my not-friends group, but the way he kept picking at his nails and pulling up his nose while we waited made me dislike him even more.

The next person to join us was Tweedy Toad, Bella's 'friend', who'd been less than polite about Jeanette and Théo's café. Tweedy came in with a woman who seemed to know him, but not like him at all, which made me take to her in an instant. She was in her forties, had very carefully coiffed blonde curls, and kept typing on a tablet. The last person to come into the hall was a cheerful Manu.

'Wonderful, everyone's here.'

I took it that meant everyone important, because both my brother and my assistant were missing from the company.

'As you can probably tell, this hall is one of the oldest parts of the château, though obviously the entrance itself has been restored in the nineteenth century in neo-Gothic style.'

I couldn't tell, and I doubted any of the others could. But Manu had lots of these little ways of making his audience feel more knowledgeable and clever than they actually were. As soon as I started paying attention to his techniques and making mental notes for my own use, I completely lost track of what he was saying about the castle. It was old. Parts of it were new. Something like that.

'New' was a relative term, of course. The bare stone walls were similar to those of most of the houses in this region, though thicker and higher, of course. But the golden yellow hue made it seem warm and light, even with the snowstorm outside blocking out daylight. Some parts of the castle had plastered walls, according to the fashion at the time of building. But a large part had been rebuilt during the reign of Louis XV, meaning that part was just as old as my brother's Maison and bits of my own house.

But you couldn't deny the grandeur of this place. The high, painted ceilings, the carved railings along balustrades and stairs, the long oriental carpets in the corridors, the wrought-iron fittings on thick oak doors: it all added up to the experience of opulence and history. A history that had started in the thirteenth century with just a *château fort*, a fortified tower that still stood to this day.

We trekked from room to room, passing the dining hall, the chapel, and the private corridor where Manu and his mother lived and paused at a large window that had been added to the *grand salon* in recent years. The air was so thick with churning snow that we couldn't make out anything but shadowy shapes.

'The weather is against us today, but I'm sure you've all seen the medieval donjon before. The cylindrical tower is the biggest of its kind for miles around and the first thing you notice when you look up at the castle. Of course, we don't need it to protect ourselves any longer. It's not going to help us deal with bridezillas.'

A polite chuckle. Manu was about to continue when a member of staff came in. He turned his back to the guests while whispering something to Manu. The smile froze on Manu's face, then slowly melted and drooped.

'I'm afraid I'll have to cut our tour short. If you go through here, you'll end up in the *petit salon. Déjeuner* is served in the dining room at twelve. Until then, feel free to explore and make yourselves at home.'

'Something wrong?' the woman with the notepad asked.

Manu hesitated. 'It seems there's a problem with the bridge.'

'You mean we're stuck?'

'There's no need to worry. We have plenty of food and every amenity. By tomorrow, I'm sure we'll have found a way to fix it. And otherwise, we'll have to pray to Saint Maurice,' he added with a laugh.

Another polite chuckle. I smiled along but had no clue as to what he was referring to. Maëline gave him a bright smile, though, before he disappeared through a side door. She did a double take when she saw my face. I've never been good at hiding my emotions.

'He meant the saint from the story,' Maëline explained.

Story? Nope, nothing came to mind. I threw my head back with an 'Ahh…' of dawning realisation, but Maëline wasn't fooled.

'You know, the story he told in that vaulted room, I can't remember what it's called…'

Feeling very dumb, I smiled apologetically.

'One of the former residents here in the Middle Ages – his name was Maurice Something-or-other – was repeatedly seen both here and in the village at the same time. So when he died, they made him a saint. You were born here. Don't they teach you the origin story in school or something?'

'Hardly. It's just another saint. Who cares. My mum is the mayor, but I don't think even she knows this story. I wonder if he just made it up.'

Maëline's eyes went round. 'He wouldn't! Would he? He seems so nice.' She stared at the door through which he'd left. 'He must have made up the ghosts, though. Don't you think? But David mentioned them too…'

Her hesitation made me laugh. I couldn't get a read on Maëline. One moment she seemed very mature and down-to-earth, the next she was full of wonder. She struck me as someone who'd read fantasy, with her earthy colours and her dreamy voice. The leggings-and-legwarmers type whom you'd expect to don a witch's hat at any moment. 'So... why is the chapel dedicated to Saint Sorlin?'

'That was done earlier. Didn't you hear anything he said?'

I guessed not. 'I know we weren't allowed into the room in the donjon that Saint Maurice supposedly occupied, because Tweedy Toad's in there now.'

Doing her best not to burst out laughing, Maëline rolled her lips between her teeth. 'You know, I heard him say it was only natural they would offer him the best room, but that he expected more of it? I don't know about yours, but mine is gorgeous.'

'Some people just cannot be pleased. You want to get some coffee? We're the last ones here.'

We went into the 'small' salon, a room at least the size of my living room, which I wouldn't have considered small before. People had gathered in groups around the space, but once again I found myself not belonging to any of them. Tweedy, a limp cigarette between his lips, was getting cosy with Sandrine over by the window. Corentin and Apolline and the nervous man were mutually boring one another by the looks of it, and the woman with the tablet was still tapping away, this time listening to a broad-shouldered, broad-bearded, frowning man in his late fifties or early sixties who looked familiar but hadn't joined us on the tour. I'd seen him before but couldn't place him. Maybe he'd come along with a client once?

By the fireplace, in a comfy chair, was my brother, pleasantly smiling at an older lady in a dark blue silk suit with an A-line skirt. She wore simple but elegant jewellery, giving her a chic, almost regal appearance. Maëline had gone straight to them and I followed.

'Ah, Julie, Maëline. This is Hélène Blanc-Mattieu, Manu's mother. My sister Julie and my... friend Maëline.'

Hélène's light blue eyes lifted to me. 'Oh, I would have known that was your sister without you telling me. Delighted to meet you, Julie. I've heard so much about you and your business already. And may I say, Maëline, what an exquisite pendant you have there. Is it Irish?'

Maëline's hand went up to her necklace. 'No, it's Celtic, but modelled after jewellery found in Bretagne. That's where I'm from.'

'How lovely.' Manu's mother engaged Maëline in a conversation about Brittany, while I pulled up a chair for her and then perched on the armrest of David's chair.

'So the bridge caved.'

'I heard.' He drank his coffee. 'Manu's really worried. They won't be able to repair it until the storm dies down, and it doesn't look like that will happen anytime soon. So this will be a much more exclusive party than expected. Aren't you glad you came?'

I know he meant it with sarcasm, but there was too much amusement in his voice. I smiled. 'Intimate. My kind of party. Made all the better, of course, by having only the cream of the crop around me. What would I do without my best friend Apolline here?'

He laughed along. Maybe he'd finally found a way to relax a little. Good, I was getting mighty fed up with my grouchy brother. David snorted, and I turned around to see what was so funny. At first I only saw Elise and Thibault entering the room, but then I noticed the matching but mirrored food stains on their shirts.

'I see you've found a way to occupy yourself?' I asked Beau when he came over.

With a smirk, Beau shrugged. 'Unless they're family or under-age, they're fair game. I don't care if they saw Cary Grant movies when they first came out.'

I rolled my eyes. 'I'm impressed you even know Cary Grant.'

'Anyone who's spent Christmas with you knows Cary Grant.'

David nodded. For some reason, he didn't seem all that averse to Thibault any more. When had that happened? I sensed a 'Let's make fun of Julie together now' coming.

Whether that was true or not, a change of course might be prudent.

'Why didn't you join us on the tour? It was very interesting.' Even if I'd only heard parts of it. 'The bedrooms alone should have given you an indication.'

Beau wasn't impressed. 'It's a bedroom. It has a bed. Job done.'

By the window a coffee cup crashed to the floor. We all turned our heads towards Marcel Carlier, who was brushing his hand over his tweed jacket.

'*Idiote!*' he hissed at Elise.

Beau tensed beside me, but Elise could handle herself.

'Sir, you bumped against me. I'd be happy to fetch you a cloth, after you apologise.'

Carlier turned purple. 'I will do no such thing. I'll fetch my own cloth and then I'll see your manager.'

He slimed off, leaving the rest of us to pretend nothing had happened.

'Hopping mad,' I mumbled to Maëline, who snorted.

Thibault brought Elise over to our little group.

'Did any of you see what happened?' she asked.

While the rest of us shook our heads, Vicomtesse Hélène said, 'No, but his behaviour towards you was intolerable. Don't worry, you'll keep your station.'

Elise smiled and thanked her, while I looked around for coffee. It seemed everyone was able to find some but me. At that point Manu entered the room, and as he passed the portrait of his great-great-probably-some-more-greats-grandfather, the similarities struck me. Tall, handsome, and immensely arrogant. Painted on his wedding day, the ancestor had greeted lookers-on with the same smug smile for centuries. His poor bride, on the other side of the door, didn't look nearly as pleased.

Yes, Manu had his little tricks of making people feel at home, but no one would ever forget that he was the king of the castle, so to speak. No wonder he and my brother got on so well. Listening to Hélène's civilised tone in speaking to her son made me think it must have been his father who'd passed on the haughty gene.

'*Voilà.*' With a wink, Elise pushed a cup of coffee into my hand.

I gave her a surprised smile. She'd gone back to serving without me noticing. And here I was thinking I kept a pretty good eye on things that happened around me. Or was she the sneaky kind? I was grateful for the drink, though, so I didn't give it another thought.

'No, I considered it,' Manu was saying to the others, 'but the wind would only blow them out. Let's just hope the temperatures don't drop much more.'

'Shame,' Maëline said. 'I'd have loved to see the fires in the vineyards. It's such a romantic sight.'

'In this weather you couldn't have seen it anyway,' David grumbled.

Manu ignored him. 'I'm glad you see the romantic side of it, but to us it's bitter necessity. Right now, the grapes are harvested and the vines have shed their leaves, so the cold will not affect them as much. Had this happened in spring, we'd be considering desperate measures. For now, though, the bridge is my first concern.'

A loud voice carried over the other conversations in the room. 'It should have been your first concern before we all came here.'

9

Fabien le Fabuleux, at your service

All eyes cut to the nervous man.

'Jérémie…' Corentin tried to hush him.

'No, no, we're all stuck here because he didn't invest in the safety of his own home. Who says the rest of the château is safe? Maybe his dad should have sold off more vineyards to pay for the upkeep of his crumbling castle.'

There was an audible intake of breath. Then a snort from Marcel Carlier. The eyes now turned to Manu. David had told me about this. Manu's dad had not been the wisest business man. Before he died, he'd sold part of the estate, but only those vineyards at the tops of the hills. The ones producing the biggest, sweetest grapes. What Manu and his mother were left with were the more vulnerable, colder parts in the valley, where in weather like this the snow gathered and threatened to freeze the vines.

Manu narrowed his eyes. 'At least my father never poisoned anyone.'

Another collective gasp. Jérémie Gümüs went bright red. He took a few slow steps as he spoke, until his lack of height had him yelling straight into Manu's chest. 'You take that back! It was never proved, and we were cleared. It's people like you bringing up the past that will be the death of me.'

Marcel Carlier now let out a full laugh. 'Oh, the irony!'

Jérémie took a step back to glare at Marcel. He opened his mouth for a retort, but closed it when Vicomtesse Hélène rose from her seat.

'I believe lunch is served.'

All three men straightened their faces and their suit jackets and filed out of the salon towards the dining room – as if they were all her children, not just Manu.

Maëline hurried to my side while exiting the salon. 'What was that all about?'

I told her what I knew about Manu's father, but I didn't know the history involved with Jérémie Gümüs. The dining room was situated next to the entrance hall, on the other side of the gallery, part of which was visible from this side as well. Round tables covered with immaculate white tablecloths ensured everyone knew the purpose of the space, but for our group the staff had set a long, rectangular table perpendicular to a stage on one side of the room.

'You're going to love this,' I heard Manu say to my brother behind me. For some reason, I didn't think he meant the food, but what else could he have in store for us?

Reaching the table, I checked the place cards for the people next to me. To my right: Jérémie Gümüs. Great. To my left and on the side of the stage: Fabien le Fabuleux. Who? It sounded like a nine-year-old magician. Turns out I was half right. The magician who took the seat next to me was a handsome, jovial man with a pencil moustache. It didn't take much for me to completely ignore the grumpy vineyard owner and focus all my attention on the newcomer.

'Hi, I'm Julie.' I gave him my most engaging smile. I felt sorry for Maëline, who sat on his left, but I needed this good-looking man's attention on me, to avoid having to talk to Jérémie. My clever opening line seemed to work. Fabien le Fabuleux turned to me with a beaming show-stopper smile.

'*Salut!* Fabien le Fabuleux, at your service. And your name is... don't tell me... something with a J. Joanne? Julie, that's it! Julie Belmain."

I was amazed. Fabien took my stunned silence as a compliment, winking at me and telling me not to ask him how I knew. I wasn't going to. My place card was right in front of me and I'd introduced myself moments before. All I could now wonder was whether it was in fact a joke, and he was making fun of my politeness. I decided to play awkward, pointing at my place card as if I'd just realised, and making an 'Ahhhh' noise with a fooled-me smile.

He winked again, pointing a finger gun at me. Oh boy. Good thing the hors d'oeuvres came out, so I could focus on a delicious trio of seafood bites. A shrimp *verrine* tempted me first, and I attacked the little glass with my tiny spoon. At the first mouthful I closed my eyes, undistractedly enjoying the fresh flavours. The world could have ended around me, and all I would know was the taste of dill and shrimp and whatever else it was that made this dish so amazing. I opened my eyes to see where Thibault was. He could always tell what was in a dish, a talent I admired and envied. They'd placed him next to my brother, across the table and to the left of me. As expected, they had their backs turned to each other, which meant that Beau was looking the other way. I'd have to remember to ask him later, and see if he could recreate it for me.

I seemed to have eaten the whole thing already. When did that happen? The choice was now between a smoked mussel on a bed of sun-dried tomato salsa and a canapé of smoked salmon mousse. Both were very good, but I longed for more of the shrimp.

'The salmon mousse is great,' Fabien informed me. 'My talent has brought me to the most wonderful places, but even in comparison, this food is really good.'

'Do you have a regular venue where you perform?'

'Oh, no. No, I get invited only. That makes me more exclusive, you see.'

And you don't have to pay rent. I mentally slapped my own fingers. His bad trick just now might have been on purpose, to break the ice. As Fabien told me about some of the places where he'd performed, I studied his face and easy manner. Play nice, Julie, you might enjoy this.

Through a delicate gourd and scallop soup and an entrée of pecorino-stuffed mushrooms, Fabien got me back on his side with little jokes and gossip about apparently famous people I'd never heard of. By the time the Thai salad with a piquant peanut dressing came around, he'd moved on to someone I did know – his current employer.

'And it turns out that all the staff, including the cook, is only hired for events such as this. They're supposed to pretend they work here all the time, but they told me they always have a lot of cleaning up to do before the guests arrive.'

I glanced at Manu over a forkful of salad. He sat across the table to my right, at the right hand of his mother, who presided at the head of the table. I supposed it made sense. If there were no events going on, it was just the two of them in this massive castle. Why pay for staff you don't need?

'So, Julie, how is your ex-husband? Have you stayed in touch at all?'

The voice made me jump. I'd made the mistake of looking right, and Jérémie had locked on.

'Not since he was convicted, no.' I hoped my voice was icy enough to deter him, but he continued.

'What exactly did he do? You know, his method?'

'Why? Do you like the idea of prison?'

He flashed me his long teeth in what I assumed was his version of a smile, but those teeth under that long, thin nose... Distinctly rodent-like.

'He was only caught because of you.'

'Thank you.' Surely he must feel the frostbite by now.

'Not long until he's released now, is it?'

'Monsieur Gümüs, let me tell you this – stay away from him and his methods. That man is dangerous.'

Jérémie let out a high-pitched chuckle. 'So am I.'

A big, fat, ghostly rat ran up my spine. All I could do was stare at the creepy man until the server's arm separated us with a plateful of meat. I stared at the venison on my plate for several long seconds, forcing down memories that would do nothing for my good mood.

'Mmm, excellent beef. Excellent blent.'

'It's...' I started, but why ruin Fabien's experience? This course came with a heady red wine that he was loving a bit too much. He was right about the meat, though. So tender it almost melted on my tongue, with a sauce just the right combination of creamy and peppery, it was, in a word, excellent.

'I can't eat this. It's too heavy.' On the far left, Marcel Carlier shoved his plate away. One of the servers hurried to his side to try and pacify him. He was too far away for me to hear the words, but the look on Vicomtesse Hélène's face said it all.

As I finished my wine, one of the staff came up to Manu and whispered something in his ear. Manu's eyebrows drew together in a look of surprised annoyance. He rose slowly from his seat, addressing the table.

'I'm afraid there is an issue with the cheese. It appears to have gone missing.'

Marcel Carlier burst out laughing. 'Well, we'll just have to stick to cheddar.'

Some of the other guests laughed along, and even Manu forced a smile. 'While I sort this out, please enjoy your desserts. May I also take this opportunity to introduce Fabien le Fabuleux! You may have heard of him, as he is a famed magician who will entertain us in a few moments. Thank you, Fabien le Fabuleux.' He led a hesitant applause that I tried to put some more life into with a whoop or two, but it only embarrassed the others more, by the looks of it. The applause died down after only a few claps.

Fabien left the table to enter the stage and direct the staff in setting up his gear, but as dessert came out at the same time, my attention was elsewhere. A range of tiny, beautifully arranged cheesecakes, macarons, bavarois, and ice creams made my mouth water. For the next few minutes, I didn't think. My world consisted of strawberry, chocolate, almond, and all kinds of other delicious flavours.

I surfaced from my pool of taste just in time to see Fabien take off his jacket and turn it inside out. It was now a silver sequinned number, from which he unbuttoned long, silver-sequinned tails. A dark purple and green paisley turban and silver-tipped walking stick completed his look.

'Ladies and gentlemen!' he began, while waving his arms in a broad gesture. 'We are about to embark on a journey of mystery and magic that will leave you stunned. Here' – another wide sweep of the arms – 'in this grand old château that has seen centuries of inhabitants going about their extraordinary lives, I will lead you to new heights of astonishment. I will...'

He paused, reaching up to his collar. 'Hang on, I've forgotten to get properly dressed.'

Taking off his turban, he swirled it around in the air a few times and spun it on his finger, but nothing especially magical happened. However, when he took it in both hands and slowly put it back on his head, a bow tie in the same fabric as the turban had appeared at his collar. His audience oohed and applauded, and Fabien took a deep bow.

I clapped along enthusiastically. His trick had surprised me, after the silly introduction and the boasting at lunch. His show might actually be good after all. I glanced around the table to see how everyone else liked the show. Closer to the stage, people had their faces turned away from me, but on the other end, our hosts were clapping. Between Jérémie and the vicomtesse sat the woman with the tablet, which she was currently without. She looked delighted. Fabien had told me she was a journalist, which made sense.

I'd also realised where I'd seen the burly man sitting next to Manu before. He was Benoît Le Roux, the mayor of Montmales, a village even smaller than Saint-Maurice. My mother had meetings with him sometimes. I now knew why I hadn't recognised him before, in the *petit salon*, when he was talking to the journalist. He'd spoken softly, whereas his usual volume was several decibels above that of a regular person. He seemed more relaxed than he'd been in the salon, and his normal tone had returned, making him instantly recognisable. I turned back to the stage and settled down deeper in my chair, wondering what would come next.

'Thank you! Yes, I was born with this. Can I get a volunteer up here for my next trick, please? The lovely young lady over there, perhaps?'

I breathed a sigh of relief when it wasn't me he was pointing at, but couldn't help a sneaky smile when I saw it was Apolline he'd picked. She did not look happy at all and shook her head, but encouraged by her husband and everyone else at the table, she couldn't gracefully say no. Her standard sour expression turned even more acidic as she pushed her chair back and dragged herself to the stage.

Fabien, meanwhile, was not helping at all with his cheers. 'Come on, you'll enjoy it. Get in the limelight. Be the limelight. You're amazing. There you go! Thanks, everyone, for making this young lady feel welcome. Give her a big round of applause! Beautiful. Now, pick a card.'

Apolline stretched out her hand, but after a few seconds of idly holding it in the air, she dropped it again. Fabien had taken out a deck of cards and was shuffling it as if his life depended on it, shooting the cards from one hand to the other, fanning them out this way and that, and making Apolline tap the deck a few times in between his manoeuvres. What that was supposed to accomplish eluded me, but in the end, he managed to get her to pick a card. More showy shuffling followed.

'Is... this!... *your* card?' With a big flourish, he drew one card from the deck and showed it to Apolline.

Apparently ready to be amazed, she first made a surprised face, but then, puzzled, she answered, 'No.'

Fabien's face fell too. 'Are... you sure?' he asked, still in his over-the-top voice.

'Quite sure.'

'Now don't be a naughty little fibber. The audience would not appreciate that.'

Neither did Apolline. Her voice went a few degrees cooler. 'It's not the same card.'

A noise on the other side of the table made me look away. David was silently shaking with laughter. Manu, as well, had his lips rolled between his teeth to keep from laughing out loud.

Fortunately, Fabien had not yet noticed their rude behaviour. 'You know what? We'll try it again.'

Oh good. Let the shuffling commence. Though I really wanted this to work for Fabien, I couldn't get into the dragged-out performance.

'Pick! Your card.'

Apolline hesitatingly pulled out a card and looked at it.

'Now please show the audience your card?'

The tiny dagger Apolline sent down her nose at Fabien before she showed her card to the audience made me feel for the man. He'd better get his trick right this time, or she was likely to simply walk off. As Apolline put her card back in the deck, Fabien looked intently at his watch, which he'd angled towards the cards. It was so obvious that it was almost painful to see. After more shuffling, he did manage to pull out the right card, but the applause was tame.

Whether Fabien noticed or not, you'd never tell by the amount of winking he did towards the audience. He continued his stories about the places where he'd performed his tricks, which was entertaining enough. It didn't distract anyone, however, from the handkerchief he dropped when he was supposed to have turned it into a dove. And everyone saw that the disappearing ball in fact went into his pocket. The magic he proclaimed to be real definitely wasn't.

By this point David and Manu had almost slipped under the table from laughing so much. I'd tried to send my brother some angry looks, but as he was seated closer to the stage than me, he would have had to glance over his shoulder to see me. To be fair, when Fabien finished his performance, David and Manu were the ones clapping and cheering the loudest.

Clueless Fabien le Fabuleux took their applause and the stunned faces of the rest of us as a mark of admiration. He bowed and grinned and bowed some more, thanking everyone and telling us what a wonderful audience we were. He even gestured to Apolline again to thank her and compliment her on being such a charming assistant.

His childlike confidence warmed my heart, even if his performance had not, so I clapped and cheered with the men across the table. Fabien blew me a kiss, which I accepted with a smile. David grinned at me, and I made a mental note to kick his plastered leg next time I got the opportunity.

10

What is wrong with you?

We vacated the dining room at half past two for a late *sieste*. No other entertainment was planned until half past three, so our little group trudged back to 'our' corridor, adjusting our pace to David's hobble.

'I'm glad you know the way,' Maëline said to him, looking up at a vaulted ceiling. 'If I were by myself, I'd probably get lost in no time. All those turrets and stairs and hidden doorways. This place is huge.'

'It's even bigger than you think. We're in one of the oldest parts of the château, but there's a whole wing back there that's not even in use any more.' David inclined his head to our right. 'Manu wants to restore it, but he needs to chat up some investors and hope he gets the grants he's applied for. He was going to do that after this whole event, but with the bridge down, there might not even be a Beaujolais Nouveau party this year.'

A framed vintage poster advertising the Beaujolais Nouveau decorated the wall in front of us as we exited the stairwell that was part of the donjon. Thibault, oblivious to my brother's worries, chuckled and stood in front of it. His body obscured part of the lettering so that the poster now read 'The Beau Nouveau Has Arrived'.

'Eyy? Come on, Juju, take my picture.'

'What? You think just because you're pretty, I'll want you in my phone?'

I whipped it out anyway to capture Thibault's cockiest pose. He never allowed me to do a shoot with him, but as long as it was him directing the poses and I didn't use them for anything, 'take my picture' were words I could expect every so often. He did like to look at himself. Even without having to do any make-up, he could take forever to get ready. Since I'm not a vain person, I could only guess what took him so long.

Checking the picture for sharpness, a line of discolouration at the edge stood out. Sure enough, the wall behind Beau was broken up by a yellow stone pilaster, next to which the paint had flaked and at intervals looked to be damp. Not the best maintenance there. But then, this castle was 750 years old. Wouldn't you have some flaky paint at that age?

Someone behind me cursed, followed by a thump. Marcel Carlier had tripped on one of the many raised doorsteps and was sprawled on the floor tiles. Thibault helped him up, but all Marcel did was curse again.

'This blasted castle is a menace! All these steps and thresholds are going to be the death of me. I already bumped my head on an arch that wasn't there before. If I didn't know better, I'd say it was haunted. Maybe that's a rumour worth spreading. Serve them right. Locking us up with negligence. I'm going to find a way to leave if it's the last thing I do.'

He was swaying on his feet as he ranted and had to grab Thibault for support more than once.

'I'm sure they'll be able to repair the bridge soon enough, Monsieur Carlier,' I said, making a show of turning to leave.

'Don't I know you?'

Apparently, he had not received the message. Repressing a sigh, I turned back to him. 'You met me yesterday in the café. Bella introduced me.'

'Who?'

As much as I couldn't stand Bella, she didn't deserve to be forgotten so quickly. Not even by Tweedy Toad. 'Pretty woman? Lives in Saint-Maurice? You had lunch with her yesterday at Jeanette Ta's place.'

I could see the wheels turning behind his watery, bloodshot eyes.

'Oh yes. She wanted to come, so I left. Nasty place, anyway.'

'Saint-Maurice? Why?'

He snorted. 'Think about it. One murder in such a small village is statistically unlikely, but two?' His shiver was for show, but his lack of control made it grotesque.

'Technically, the second was an accident,' Beau said.

'Technically, you now live in a dangerous area. But maybe you like consorting with criminals?'

There was no way he'd know about Beau's family, but his inadvertent hit had Beau's jaw muscles working.

'Can we help you to your room, Monsieur Carlier?' Maëline offered. The rest of us tried not to look too disappointed that she had to be helpful. Carlier had no such reservations.

'You think I'm senile? I can get myself to my room, girl. I suppose you want to join me, but I have made other plans. Besides, this is my room.'

He waddled to the door opposite the framed poster. 'Now shove off, I don't want you making noise outside when I'm trying to sleep.'

David was already halfway through the corridor. We quickly followed him, which meant we all ended up in David's room. Maëline fussed over his leg until he reluctantly sat down and put it up on a stool.

'What a nasty man,' I said, holding on to one of the posters of the bed, still feeling the after-effects of Tweedy Toad's cold slime.

A silent nod from the others was all the answer I got. I must not be the only one who felt it.

Thibault wrinkled his nose. 'I'd rather sit through one of Fabien le Fabuleux's shows again than talk to Carlier.'

David burst out laughing, which irritated me.

'Did you have to be so rude during his show?' I asked my brother.

He gave me a big grin. 'His show was never going to be good. Manu would have made sure of that.' He wiggled his head, realising that comment needed more explanation. 'When he was little, Manu thought he should be a magician. You know, because of his different-coloured eyes? He thought it would make him stand out. So he tried to learn tricks and he was so... *so* bad. He knew how everything worked, but he couldn't get the sleight of hand right. Never made it. So now, every time one of us finds a clip of bad magic online, we send it to each other. I think he'd already booked this guy before I told him I'd be on holiday.'

I humphed. 'I still think you shouldn't have been so rude as to laugh in his face.'

David jerked his upper body towards me. 'Did you *see* him? He had no clue! He was smiling and thanking us and saying how glad he was that we'd enjoyed the show so much. Man, the guy was so full of himself, I could have booed him and he'd taken it as a compliment.'

'Probably true,' Thibault chimed in. 'He really didn't need all your flirting to boost his ego any further.'

'My fl—!' I started, but stopped when everyone was nodding. Instead, I humphed again.

'You're a huge flirt,' Beau continued.

'Look who's talking! *Loulou*.'

He was unfazed. 'This guy, though. I mean, why? Do you actually like him?'

I glared at him for a second. 'I think he's absolutely...' But then I couldn't keep my face straight and laughed. 'He is rather pompous, isn't he? Seriously, Beau, you should know me better than that.'

Maëline grinned along. 'He's handsome, though. Don't you want to try one of those moustaches, Beau?'

Thibault twirled the tip of a non-existent moustache, but David moped.

'Too many "attractive" men around here.'

'Well, he is. Manu, I mean,' Maëline added, nodding at me. Must have been one of the positive things she'd mentioned to David when he asked what she thought of his friend.

I nodded. I could see the attraction. He wasn't my type – a bit too long and thin in the face – but his easy smile made up for a lot.

'Apparently, his best friend is some kind of bluebeard, and every door I open in this château will have unsuspecting exes rolling out of it.'

'I only said…' David's dark eyes went cold. 'Forget it. My foot hurts. I think I'll stay in my room for dinner.'

Maëline pressed her lips together. But her voice remained soft and calm. 'Remind me, how did you break your ankle, again?'

He narrowed his eyes. 'Skiing.'

'Oh, so you do have fun sometimes. If you don't need me right now, perhaps you'll excuse me.'

As she left the room, Beau and I exchanged a glance.

'You could be nicer to her,' Beau said.

'We don't all flirt with every skirt,' was the grunted answer.

'No, but even you are not normally this much of a pr—'

'Beau!' Though I agreed with the sentiment, this was not the time to start a fight.

'I'll see you later, Juju.'

He left too, and I glared at my brother. 'What is wrong with you?'

'I broke my ankle.'

'Ha. Ha. Do you have to take your annoyance with your own clumsiness out on Maëline?'

'She shouldn't be here, and that's your fault.'

'She was invited, same as you and me.'

'She wouldn't have been there to *be* invited if it weren't for you. Now Manu's going to sweep her off her feet and she'll be yesterday's news before you know it.'

I pinched the bridge of my nose. 'David… that happened once. You forgave him long ago, so get over it. Besides, that was a girl you were in love with. You said you don't even like Maëline! What's it to you if she falls for Manu?'

'She shouldn't be here! I don't need her. Not in the house and not here. And she looks like she walked straight out of a fantasy novel with those earthy tones and capes and stuff. She's that felted type of person. You know, macramé and wildflowers. A hippie.'

'What's wrong with hippies? Some people just want to be free.'

'Says the person who considers hairspray a necessity of life. She wears leg warmers, for crying out loud!'

A rustle at the door had us both biting our lips.

11

Magical in its devastation

Maëline glanced down at her leg warmers. Okay, not everyone wore them any more, but she liked them. Who was he to judge her because of them? This was ridiculous. Free roof or not, she wasn't going to be insulted for it. She'd call her boss as soon as she'd blown off some steam.

Stomping through the corridor, she flexed her hands into fists and stretched them again. Why had she lingered? She should have just gone back to her room. Thibault had been sweet when he came out, but had left her with a little shoulder squeeze when she didn't react. She still didn't know what to make of him. He was so over the top most of the time that it was difficult to take him seriously.

She turned another corner, descended a few steps, then realised she was in an unfamiliar hallway. Huh. Was this not the way to the dining room? She was pretty sure she'd gone in the right general direction. Maybe, if she turned left at the end of this corridor, she would be somewhere near the kitchen.

Probably. Only, at the end of the corridor there was nothing but a spiral staircase going up.

Maëline shrugged. What difference did it make if she went to the dining room or not? She'd only chosen to go there because she'd seen it before and thought she knew the way. She passed a door marked *Privé* that was left open. Had it been any other door, she'd only have given it a cursory glance. But this door was different. It was Private. But also not, because it was open. As paradoxes go, this one was irresistible, and she peeked inside.

It was empty. Was that lucky or disappointing? She couldn't decide. After all, the room was pretty boring. A desk, a laptop, some stationery, an empty coffee cup. Old books on the shelves that didn't look like they were ever read. Ledgers that looked like they were. Must be Manu's office.

Wondering whether she'd calmed down enough to tell her boss to find someone else to babysit David, Maëline turned around and started further down the corridor. More Private rooms, but they were all closed. The corridor curved to the right just when she'd decided that if she went left at every turn, she would probably end up somewhere she'd already been and then could find her way back. If all else failed, she could always turn around, but this early in, that felt like cheating.

At the end of the curve, daylight came in through windows half covered in snow. Maëline rubbed her arms. These outside walls might be thick, but there wasn't any other kind of insulation, and the last radiator she'd passed was quite a while back. There wasn't even any carpet in this corridor. Maybe she should turn back after all.

Of course, that was the moment she encountered another open door. Looking over her shoulder but not really expecting anyone there, she pushed the door open further. A little swirl of dust blew out around her feet. Maëline's mouth fell open as she entered the room. David had mentioned that there was a part of the castle that wasn't in use any more, but he hadn't said it was this... abandoned. Wallpaper billowed off the walls like curtains. Part of the ceiling had collapsed, leaving a pile of broken wood, sand, and bits of plaster in one corner of the room. One of the beams had broken a window, allowing in wind and, with it, plant seeds. Various bits of greenery had already found their home on the pile of rubble – ferns, grass, and even a beech sapling.

She touched the leaves of the young tree, finding the whole place magical in its devastation. Nature reclaiming a building that was still lived in. Though the cold was slowly seeping into her bones, the dust particles inside mimicking the snow outside filled her with a kind of warmth. Despite the gale, the peaceful quietness in this room was so natural that she thought she could stay here forever.

'Who are you?'

Maëline jumped back as if stung at the unexpected sound of a woman's voice. Bedecked in a woollen scarf, hat, and mittens, a tall young woman stared at Maëline through dark, wary eyes. Her skin was very pale, enhanced by the white clothing she wore, but from underneath the hat peeped a lock of black hair.

'A guest! I'm one of Manu's guests. I'm sorry if I'm not supposed to be here, but I didn't think I'd be in anybody's way.'

'You're trespassing,' the woman stated, standing still as a statue. Her mouth must have moved, but it was hidden by the chunky scarf.

'I'm sorry.' What else could she say? She fidgeted with her nails, now fully feeling the cold in the room.

'So am I.' The woman finally moved, gesturing with her mittened hand for Maëline to come away from the window. 'Trespassing, I mean. And sorry. Come, the next room is warmer.'

Not knowing what to make of that confession, Maëline followed her to the next room. It was slightly less demolished, the ceiling and windows being intact. In the corner furthest from the windows and the door sat what looked like a kind of nest made from a mouldy mattress and old swathes of fabric.

'You... live here?' *Please say no.* There had been far too much talk of ghosts in the last couple of days. This woman-in-white was making her quite uneasy. But then, the style of her clothing would make her a very recent ghost. Was that realisation supposed to make her feel better? Because it didn't.

'No! Well...'

Maëline braced herself. She had no roof. The last thing she'd done before getting lost was upset the owner of her temporary roof. Was this her future?

'I was taking pictures...' The woman pulled a big, black, decidedly real camera from between the folds of her layers and held it up in evidence. 'For my urbex blog. And then the snow hit. I thought I could sit it out for a day or so, but then in come all these people, and there was no way I could get out unseen. I should have realised there'd be Beaujolais Nouveau festivities, but hey, I'll never win an award for planning. You wouldn't happen to have something to eat on you, would you?'

Maëline shook her head.

'I've been taking food from the kitchen at night, but last night there were these guys there... I got back here as fast as I could, but you've no idea how hungry I am.'

'I'm sorry. I was trying to find the dining room, but I got lost. Would it not be... easier, if you just came clean and told them you were here?'

The woman's eyes widened. 'No, man! I'd ruin this place for other urbexers. They'd put up security or something.'

'I'm sorry, urbex?'

'Urban exploration. Like, we go into abandoned places and take pictures. Just photos, you know, never anything destructive. We leave the place just as we find it. It's kinda spooky.' She smiled behind her scarf but then her eyes widened and her gaze shot from left to right. 'Nowhere near as creepy as this place, though. I think it's legit haunted! I've never heard sounds like that before. Once, I was this close to just running into the house, man. But then I thought, hey, they're spirits. What are they gonna do, right? So I set up camp here, closer to the civilised world, so I don't hear them so loud.'

Ghosts, again? On cue, the wind howled in the chimney, making both women jump.

'Not like that, though. More like, as if there's people talking in the next room, but then you go and look, and there's nobody there. Like they're in the walls.' Her eyes wide, she hugged herself as she spoke.

Maëline told herself she did not believe in ghosts – not really – and also that she was going to get out of here, now.

'So... have you heard that the bridge is out? You could be stuck here for a while. Are you sure you don't want to confess?'

The woman stared at her nest, obviously conflicted. 'I'd rather not. I guess it depends on how much longer, though. Do you think you could maybe bring me some food?'

Come back here after she'd managed to get away? But her tendency to help won out. 'I can try... I only ended up here because I got lost. I haven't even been to the kitchen, so...'

The woman held up her mitten. 'Hang on, I'll draw you a little map. It's not hard once you know where to go.' She picked up a backpack and rummaged through it. 'I'm Sacha, by the way. Sacha Toledo. Here.' She sketched out some lines, arrows, and crosses on a piece of paper, then led Maëline out of the room. 'Follow the corridor back to the warm bit, then right, down the stairs, two more rights, and you're at the back of the dining room. That's this X. Pass that, left, right, there's the kitchen.' The tip of her pencil tapped the other X.

Maëline took the paper and nodded. 'All right. I'll make sure—'

A faint sound echoed down the corridor. Maëline and Sacha shared an alarmed look.

'Was that a scream?'

12

No body, no murder

The ear-piercing scream stopped me from chewing David out over his behaviour.

'Maëline!' was his first reaction.

I frowned. 'I don't think so...'

Thibault threw open the door. 'What was that?'

'Stay here!' I barked at my brother when he got up.

'I can help.'

'Possibly, but Maëline is bound to come here after that scream, and you need to be here to apologise. I'll come back for you if we need you.' I'd crossed the room and joined Beau at the door. 'Left, I think.'

He nodded, and we hurried over the thick carpets down several corridors until we met more worried-looking people. Corentin and Apolline Bailly came from the opposite direction, both performing a quasi-dignified run-walk. Corentin took the lead, heading off to where excited voices sounded.

'Isn't this Carlier's room?' Beau asked when we halted in front of the vintage poster he'd posed at before. Almost all the other guests had arrived and formed a ring around Sandrine Lardy, who was sobbing loudly against the much smaller journalist's shoulder. The poor woman was trying to calm Sandrine down, but with the amount of dramatic noise Sandrine made, she was desperately out of her league.

Before I could make a move, Beau stepped in. He took Sandrine from the little woman and had her sobbing quietly against his shoulder in no time. Still, even he couldn't get a sensible word out of her for the first minute or so. Jérémie and the mayor of Montmales had shrugged and retreated by then.

'Dead!' she finally wailed. That got all our attention.

'Who's dead?' Apolline asked, eyeing me suspiciously.

'Marcel!'

I immediately turned and knocked on his door. No answer.

'He can't open, he's dead!' Even in this state, she clearly implied the words 'you moron'.

I tried the door handle, just to be sure, but knelt down to look through the keyhole when the door remained closed. All the doors locked with old-fashioned keys, so I should have been able to at least see some light come through. But what I saw was... nothing. The keyhole was completely dark.

Sandrine whimpered against Beau's shoulder.

I turned my face up to her. 'Excuse me, but... why do you think he's dead?'

She turned, her face blotchy and smeared with mascara. 'Are you blind? He's right there, on the floor, with a great big antler sticking out his back.'

I recoiled and cast another glance through the keyhole, but with the same result. Corentin knelt next to me, and I gave him room to look, but he shrugged too. 'Can't see a thing.'

'What's going on?'

Panting, Manu ran up to us, melting snow dripping from his hair onto his black wool coat, where it formed dark patches. He'd probably been checking on the bridge and hadn't heard the scream.

'Marcel is dead!' Sandrine screeched.

'She says she saw him through here, but it's blocked,' Corentin explained. 'Do you have a spare key?'

Manu hesitated. 'I must have one somewhere... I'd have to check.'

I looked at Thibault, who shook his head the tiniest bit, but Manu still noticed. 'Think you can help?'

'Well... I could, but... I mean... privacy and all...'

'I'd say we have good cause to check the room, don't you?' Corentin asked.

Manu agreed and invited Beau to do his thing. For a moment, I wondered how Manu would know about

Thibault's background, but David must have told him. Proof, once again, that guys gossip just as much as girls.

Handing Sandrine back to the journalist, Thibault took something out of his pocket and set to work on the door, which opened in a matter of seconds.

'Careful!' I couldn't help myself saying as he opened the door and stepped inside.

After a quick look around, he reached around the door and pulled a cloth handkerchief from the keyhole. Then he pushed the door open further so we could all see. The room was empty, save from the usual furniture. A suitcase stood open on the luggage rack, but nothing seemed out of the ordinary.

Sandrine staggered inside, her eyes wide, pointing down to a spot on the parquet floor. 'He was right here! On a rug. Bleeding.'

'With an antler in his back,' Corentin added with no small amount of sarcasm.

'An antler?' Manu pulled up an eyebrow in disbelief, and Sandrine nodded. 'Well, he clearly is not here now, so I don't think we need to worry about it. I'm sure he'll turn up.'

'Is something wrong?'

'*Maman.*' Manu closed his eyes a fraction too long. 'Nothing of concern. Already taken care of.'

'Madame Lardy thought she saw a murdered man, but as you can see, she must have been mistaken.' Apolline had taken on some of her husband's sarcasm in that explanation. They both shrugged and returned to their room.

Vicomtesse Hélène gasped, frowning at her son with more worry than surprise. 'Murder? Monsieur Carlier?'

'There is no murder, *maman*. Look, the room is empty. I'll take you back to your room and have someone bring up a *tisane*. Herbal tea will do you good.'

She stood a little straighter. 'Don't patronise me, Manu. Have them bring one for Madame Lardy instead. Come, my dear, you must have had a shock.' She took Sandrine by the shoulders and led her away from the upsetting room.

Manu hesitated, but then followed. 'Thibault, could I ask you...?'

Beau nodded and closed the door, while Manu disappeared down the hallway. 'Well, that was a lot of fuss over nothing,' he mumbled, locking the door once more.

I shrugged. 'I know Sandrine can be overly dramatic, but she seemed genuinely upset. The thing I'm wondering is, why was she here in the first place?'

A tiny gasp reminded us that the little journalist was still there. We both blinked at her, and she gave a little wave. 'Thank you for taking care of her,' she said to Beau. She spoke softly, but without the soothing qualities Maëline's gentle voice possessed. 'I tried to calm her, but she was hysterical.'

'No problem. I'm Thibault Fouquet.' He stretched out his hand, which she took with a giggle. Huh. She hadn't seemed like the type to giggle at Beau. Her manner had been professional up till now, and her eyes, behind rectangular black-rimmed glasses, didn't miss much. But her long blonde hair shone a little too much for ordinary care, and she wore a pink, fluffy cardigan. That must be the giggle part of her.

'Romy Martin. I write for *Le Courant*. You think she was supposed to meet Carlier in his room?' She still had her Beau-smile on when she addressed me. The giggle part and the professional part worked in unison. I couldn't help but like this woman.

'I can't honestly comment on that. But why would she be at this corner if not to meet him? Did she say anything before we arrived?'

Romy shook her head. 'I happened to be just around the corner when she screamed. She came running my way, flailing her arms and pointing behind her. I'd only just managed to get her back here when you came.'

Thibault pulled his mouth to one side. 'That makes it less likely to be a distraction for something else. If she wanted people to come here, why run away?'

'A... distraction?' Romy's eyes flicked between Beau and me.

'Never mind him. He's solving a murder before there even is one.'

Her eyes widened and her index finger flicked from one of us to the other. 'Oh, that's right. You were the ones that found that old lady's killer. You really think there's been another murder?'

'Well—' Beau started, but I cut him off with a pointed stare.

'No body, no murder. Right? Carlier said it himself – it's statistically unlikely.'

'I'd still love to interview you, though. I know you didn't want to talk to the press, but with this new mystery taking place...?'

Wishing Jacqueline, my friend in the police force, had taken credit like I told her to, I said, 'I think it's time for us to go to the conference room. It's twenty past three.'

'Oh, right, the presentation.' Beau wrinkled his nose. 'But that's not for us. That's for investors and other business partners. I feel wildly out of place as it is. I mean, it's nice that Manu invited us, but I don't think he intended to.'

I knew exactly what he meant. I still had trouble fitting in around the people in the village where I was born and raised, so among the so-called crème de la crème of the Beaujolais, I felt like I was constantly on my toes. All I wanted was a good cuddle with my cat Henri, but instead, we accompanied Romy to the conference room. It would be interesting to see what the others made of the situation, and besides, what else was there to do?

'You didn't get an official invitation?' Romy pushed her glasses up.

'Hardly. Manu came by her brother's yesterday and more or less told us all to come.'

Romy lapped it all up. I tried to catch Beau's attention to make him stop talking. With reporters, everything was on record. Though Manu was David's friend and not mine, you never knew how your innocent words could be twisted into something that hurt someone else. And if the someone employed lots of people, you wouldn't want to be the cause of trouble.

'David had an official invitation. He was supposed to be on holiday, though. So when he broke his ankle and had to return home, Manu renewed his invitation. That's not so strange. We just happened to be there, and he was generous enough to include us.' There. That was all positive and could not be twisted.

We took seats in the back, where David was already sipping wine.

'You're a bad influence. One look at you, and people start seeing murders everywhere.'

Deciding he wasn't worth the negative energy, I ignored him and stared at the promotional video showing on a big screen for a few minutes, until it started again. By then, most of the seats had been taken. Elise and some other personnel went round with drinks, serving everyone with a smile. When Sandrine came in, all eyes cut to her, but Elise simply led her to a chair and brought her a glass of wine. Obviously aware of people's stares, Sandrine kept her eye on her glass, taking little sips and checking her phone every two seconds.

Still three thirty-five, huh? I realised I'd been checking the time too. Weren't we supposed to start at half past three? The Baillys, Corentin and Apolline, all the way at the front, were turning in their seats to see who was missing. As far as I could see, though, only Marcel Carlier's chair was empty.

'Ladies and gentlemen,' Manu started, 'as you can see, we are waiting for one more person to arrive. I'm sure he has his reasons for not showing, but Julie, might I ask you to bring my mother here instead?'

I nodded and rose, while Manu continued, 'Though she doesn't participate in many of the social events any more, she still has an active interest in the business and...'

The rest of it was lost to me when I closed the door of the conference room behind me. I looked around, trying to remember the way to the family's private quarters. Maybe I should have asked Manu to refresh my memory, but in the end, I only got lost once and I realised it quickly enough to return and try again.

Turning into the family's corridor, I did breathe a little sigh of relief, though. Now which door would be the vicomtesse's?

I stretched my fist out to the nearest door to knock but jumped when the carpet squelched underfoot. Stepping to the side, I raised my hand again and knocked. If this was the state of the plumbing, no wonder Manu needed investors.

'Enter.'

It was the vicomtesse's voice, so I must have picked the right door. I stuck my head around it. 'Manu asks if you would like to join us for the presentation?'

'Oh! Err... Come in, come in.' She waved me into a room with light, feminine furniture that looked very modern and, frankly, out of place in an ancient castle. 'Yes, I suppose... Yes, I would like that.' She glanced around distractedly, and I noticed a greasy stain on her skirt that hadn't been there earlier. But then Madame Blanc-Mattieu composed herself. 'Yes. Thank you.'

She followed me out of the room, locked it behind her, and would have accompanied me to the conference room, when a thought struck me.

'Would you mind going by yourself, Madame? I'd like to check Monsieur Carlier's room one more time.' Tweedy Toad might be a nasty little man, but if Manu had invited him here, he must need his help. Since he'd invited me, too, I felt obliged to do my bit to get his leaky castle fixed.

A sliver of her earlier worry crept over the vicomtesse's face, but she overcame it with grace. 'Of course. Thank you, Madame Belmain.'

Great. Now I had to go deal with an arrogant toad and drag him off to somewhere he didn't want to be. Thanks, Mum, for raising me too well. Dragging my feet, I lumbered back to the tower room and knocked. And knocked again. Well, he wasn't here. Too bad. Sorry, Manu, I've done my duty. Now I could go sit through a boring presentation with a clean conscience. Then why was I crouching in front of the keyhole?

I looked and leaned back on my heels. Then I shot off a text to Thibault.

He's back. He's dead. There's an antler.

13

Tell me what to do

The first to arrive was Manu, white as a sheet. He was followed closely by Thibault, who opened the door but stayed on the threshold to prevent everyone else from entering the room. One by one they bumped into him to see the spectacle.

He turned around with a deep frown that was rare for him. 'What is wrong with you all? This isn't a TV show. A man has died. Show some respect.'

They all took a few steps back at that, but most were still craning their necks to get a glimpse of the man lying on the rug in the middle of the room, an antler sticking out of his back.

'Julie, I don't have much time.' My phone showed the face of Jacqueline, slightly irritated that I'd call her instead of the other way round. Because of her irregular schedule, we'd agreed she'd do the calling. But this was an exception.

'I think you'll have time for this.' I switched to the back camera and filmed over Beau's shoulder.

'Is that...? Where are you?'

'Château de Montmales. The bridge is out, and someone has been murdered.'

There was a silence, followed by a quickly suppressed groan. 'You're sure he's dead?'

'I haven't checked. I didn't want to disturb the crime scene, and he was seen before, only… he… sort of disappeared. But now he's back. But I don't think he's alive. Because the rug had disappeared too, *tu vois*?'

Jacqueline stared open-mouthed at her phone. '*D'accord.* Well, go in and don't touch anything other than what is necessary to check his vitals.'

Thibault stepped to the side, and I entered the room, both hands holding my phone to make sure I wouldn't touch anything. I swallowed as I neared Marcel's body. Yes, I'd helped solve a murder not too long ago, but I hadn't actually seen the body then. This was making the whole thing a lot more real. Marcel was face down on the fluffy oval rug, his hands extended above his head. The single antler, its mount still attached, was buried in the middle of his back. I angled the phone so Jacqueline could see, but tried not to look at it myself. I hunched down to feel Marcel's pulse, first at his wrist, then at his throat, but he was dead all right.

'He's dead,' I specified to Jacqueline.

She sighed. 'Know who he is?'

'Marcel Carlier. He was a guest here as well, but I don't actually know what he does. Did.'

'All right.' Her computer keyboard rattled. She nodded at someone off-camera. 'Go back out. Send everyone away for now, but leave Beau at the door. Get your camera and your gloves and any kind of protective gear you can think of, like a scarf over your mouth and hair. Ask if they have some plastic bags for your shoes. Call me back when you're ready.'

Ending the call, I took a deep breath. Now that I'd done what my brain had told me to do, my emotions fought their way to the front. The hair on my arms raised, and my knees buckled. Leaning against the door frame to keep my balance, I glanced round the circle of expectant faces. Why did they look to me for guidance? I had no idea what to do either! 'It's probably best if you all return to your rooms—'

'What?' Sandrine exclaimed. 'With a murderer on the loose? I don't think so.'

'All right, then go back to the conference room. I'll let you know what we're supposed to do as soon as they tell me.'

Eyeing each other suspiciously, everyone slinked back to where they came from. David, the only one aside from Sandrine who did not rush forward to get a glimpse of Marcel, shook his head. 'You were always the troublemaker.'

'I'm sorry? *I* didn't kill anyone.'

He looked surprised. 'No, no, I meant you were always the troublemaker and now look at you. You have the *ton* of the southern Beaujolais doing what you tell them to. I'm impressed.'

He hobbled off, but his compliment baffled me more than the dead man in the room behind me.

Thibault grinned at my expression. 'Underhanded compliments. I guess you're related after all.'

I shook myself out of my astonishment and returned to my room to fetch my gloves and camera.

An antler to the back. My stomach roiled. Much as I disliked the man, nobody deserved that. Who would do such a thing? And at a party! In my head, I went round the table at lunch to consider all of the guests, but none of them stood out as a likely suspect. That didn't comfort me one bit, though. Someone in this castle was a murderer, and if I didn't know who, I'd likely be scared of all of them until the killer was found.

From my bedroom window, I could see the snow still whirling around the castle. There was no way Jacqueline was going to get here through that weather. Instructing me to go in and take pictures was her way of telling me that. But it also meant that whoever had killed Carlier would not be arrested until much later. Because they'd have to find him or her first. Unless I maybe...?

Oh, no. Not that again. Last time I got involved, it had turned out all right. But what if this time the killer decided to go after me? There was nowhere to go! I was still muttering 'no' to myself by the time I reached Beau. He was leaning against the wall next to the door, one knee bent, foot pushed up against the wall. His thumbs were racing across the screen of his phone.

'Don't tell me you're on social media.'

'Just texting Céline. What do you take me for? But I did check, and so far, everyone has been smart enough to stay off social media. No mentions of murder yet. Only some moaning from people who were supposed to come to the party on Thursday but can't because of the weather. I'd feel bad for Manu, if he didn't already have a murder in his home to worry about.'

I made a face. 'Poor man. Unless he did it, of course.'

Beau snorted. 'Yeah, right. Let me murder someone in my own house, right before my own super-important party. Also, wasn't this guy supposed to give him lots of money?'

'I don't know. Guess we'll have to find out.' I wrinkled my nose, but Thibault's eyes lit up.

'Of course! The police can't get here, so we'll have to do the interviews. Which do you want to be, good cop or bad cop?'

'Beau...' I groaned. Not this again. No, no, no. With a sigh, I called Jacqueline, who answered immediately.

'I've tried, Juju, but all routes are cut off. I'll have to do this remotely. I'm sorry.'

Yep, that's what I thought. I nodded. 'Okay, so tell me what to do.'

'First, tell me what happened as you yourself have experienced it.'

I related what we'd been doing from the moment we arrived at the castle. I thought that would cover everything, but then I had to go back to yesterday and explain how we got to be invited. When I got to the part where there was supposed to be a murder but without a body, Jacqueline frowned. She asked me several more questions, but I could only repeat what I'd already said. I continued my story, ending with finding the body after all.

'In the same position the other woman' – she checked her notes – 'Sandrine Lardy had seen it before?'

'I assume so. She didn't say there was anything different, but she may not have looked the second time.'

'All right.' More notetaking. 'Thibault, I'll talk to you later, but is there anything you'd like to add?' When he said no, she continued, 'Let's start with the photos, then. We'll need a good impression of the scene and the body, so you'll need to send us pictures of that. Then afterwards, you'll have to go and talk to everyone in the building, but I'll tell you what to pay attention to when you're doing that later. Perhaps someone could set up an interview room?' While Beau nodded and reached for his phone, Jacqueline continued, 'Tie up your hair, put on your gear, and get to work.'

I saluted and did as she told me. Police-Jacqueline is scary. Still on the call, I asked Beau to let me in, and he unlocked the door.

'You locked it again?'

He shrugged. 'It's only polite.'

'Thibault, what kind of lock is it?' Jacqueline asked. I pointed the camera at Beau, who recoiled. Like I said, police-Jacqueline is scary.

'Simple lever lock. Hardly a lock at all.'

'Hm.' The keyboard rattled again.

'You mean, it's easy to get in?' I asked.

'Don't leave any valuables in your room,' Beau said.

'How about myself, when I go to sleep tonight?'

He had no answer to that.

'Ready, Julie?'

I lifted my phone and gave a thumbs-up.

'All right. Before you go in, check for footprints or any other evidence on the floor. Make sure you don't walk all over it. Then go in and take as many pictures as you can, first of the room and then of the body itself. Don't forget the door and the lock. Has anybody else been inside the room?'

'Just me,' I said, entering and taking in the rest of the room fully for the first time. 'That is, after the body returned. When Sandrine announced the murder, everyone went inside to check that there was, in fact, no murder. Or no body. Not there, in any case. *Punaise*, this is complicated.'

A big four-poster bed took up most of the space. Two large windows on either side showed the storm going strong, but the wind was blowing up against this side of the castle and most of the glass was covered with snow. The wall on the left was lined with bookshelves and an ancient built-in desk underneath a little cupboard with leaded glass doors. On the right, a wardrobe riddled with woodworm holes was overshadowed by an enormous tapestry of a hunting scene. It was a floor-to-ceiling kind of affair in muted colours, fraying on the edges. The parquet flooring showed quite a bit of wear, but rugs on either side of the bed covered up the worst parts. At the foot of the bed stood the luggage rack with Marcel Carlier's open suitcase. And then there was, of course, the salmon-coloured rug that the man himself currently occupied.

I switched on the lights, leaned my phone against a porcelain ornament on the antique desk, and clicked off a few general shots to establish the dimensions of the space. I was already getting hot with all the extra layers Jacqueline had me put on and I hadn't even come close to photographing the body yet. To be honest, I was putting it off. The fact that I wouldn't be asking Marcel to give me a cheeky smile made my stomach turn.

I photographed every bit of the room – the phone on the bedside table, the files on the desk, the shoes underneath the luggage rack. Using every trick I could think of, I showed their relation to other objects and possible significance in the crime scene. I even opened the wardrobe and photographed it open and closed, just to be thorough. It didn't seem big enough to hide a grown man, especially one with... an expanded girth, as one side of the wardrobe was fitted with shelves. Eventually, though, I couldn't put it off any longer.

'When you're shooting the victim, get up close.'

Great.

'Make sure you capture the scene from their level as well.'

I hunched down in my thick winter gear, folding in blobs of down and wool to get a better angle. Once I made myself get over the fact that there was an antler sticking out of a man's back, I had the pictures done quite quickly. I'd already paid particular attention to the face, hands, and feet, but Jacqueline had me go over them again in search of specific jewellery or body markings.

'There aren't any. Except if you count the fact that he should have changed his socks a few days ago. They don't look dirty, but there's this weird smell around him. So, what's next? We can't just leave him there. Do we... sort of... make him more comfortable? Put him on the bed or something?'

'Well... ordinarily we'd want you to disturb as little as possible, but under these circumstances... it would probably be best if you wrapped him in a clean sheet and left him in a cold place. A spare fridge, or even the snow outside.'

'You know that could be days, right?'

'It's the best we can do.'

I supposed she was right, but it felt wrong leaving a man, even one as nasty as Marcel Carlier, lying in the snow with an antler in his back. Still, it was probably better than leaving him in a warm room for several days.

'Can you see anything that's out of place? A fallen pair of scissors, hair or fibre that shouldn't be there, maybe blood spatter?'

I swallowed. 'Other than what's on him and the rug, no.'

'Okay, then you're almost done.'

That was a relief. Much as I was willing to do what was necessary, I could only be alone in a room with a dead person so long before it got to me. And it was getting to me.

'Do you have those plastic bags?'

'I had two ziplock bags in my camera bag, but I used them to cover my feet.'

'Ask them to bring you some more and bag the files from the desk. Now... there's one more thing...'

Oh no. Here it comes.

'We need to make sure there's no evidence underneath him or in his pockets that the killer could later remove. You'll have to check his pockets and look underneath the body.'

'Can't I do that when they take him outside?'

'We can't risk the killer removing anything unseen.'

I whimpered. Taking his picture was one thing. Actually touching him? I'd have to burn my gloves afterwards. Yes, I know I touched him before, when I was checking his vitals, but that was when I thought he might still be alive. Call me squeamish if you like, I don't care. I'm not comfortable touching a dead person. I texted David, asking him to have some plastic bags and a clean sheet brought up, but then there was no more putting it off.

Using only my finger and thumb, I pulled Marcel's jacket to the side and checked the pockets. Nothing there. His trouser pockets only held his wallet and a dirty handkerchief. Taking a deep breath, I then rolled him over enough to quickly check underneath him, but when there was nothing there, I lowered him back and did a little hop around the room, flapping my hands in a fruitless effort to forget what I'd just done.

'I saw that. You'd make a lousy policewoman.'

'That's why I'm a photographer. Of happy faces.' I took a few more deep breaths. Beau handed me the plastic bags at the door, which I used to secure the files from the desk, as well as

Marcel's phone and wallet. Then I picked up my own phone and almost ran out of the room. Let's never do that again.

Of course, Thibault had witnessed the whole scene, too, but he was wise enough to keep to a grin. While I received more instructions from Jacqueline, he helped me out of my coat and rubbed my back. He's a good guy, after all. A feeling that disappeared the moment he put his arm around my shoulders and moved himself into the video call.

'Anything I can do?' he asked. 'I still have this handkerchief I pulled out of the keyhole.'

'It's quite similar to the one Carlier has in his pocket,' I said, glancing up while taking the bags off my shoes.

'Then it's probably taken from him, but show it to the other guests nonetheless. Maybe one of them will have a reaction to it. Thibault, while Julie uploads her pictures, you and one or two of the others will have to remove the body and place it somewhere cold. Then see if you can set up one or two interview rooms. We can ask the questions over a video call, but we won't be able to pick up on all the body language, so we need one of you there in each room. We are working on getting to you, but it won't be today. Julie, can you take a few photos of the corridor outside the room, too, please? Call me back when you're ready to do the interviews.'

Looking over my shoulder at the closed door, I shivered.

Thibault rubbed my arms. 'You did really well.'

I huffed. 'He's still in there.'

'I know, but there's nothing we can do for him now, except help find the person who killed him.'

I sighed. 'And make sure they don't do it again.' I took some last shots of the corridor and folded up my tripod, when Manu arrived with Benoît Le Roux, the mayor of Montmales. Beau unfolded the sheet, and I got out of there to find a computer.

14

I thought I was going crazy

The conference room, another painted and gilded number made modern with office chairs and a giant screen on one end, was now largely empty. The vicomtesse had invited everyone to the more comfortable intimacy of the *petit salon*, leaving the conference room the best place to conduct our interviews. Though people were bound to be nervous when interrogated by a larger-than-life Jacqueline, it felt more official than showing them a phone. The camera set up with the TV caught more of the people present than a phone camera could, too, allowing Jacqueline and her colleagues to pick up more of the body language.

Since Beau was still taking care of Carlier, though, I used my time here to upload my photos and call Jacqueline to make sure the connection was all right. She was in a different room now, surrounded by more of her colleagues. Her second-in-command, Marc Froment, sat just out of reach of their camera, but I saw half his expressionless face move in and out of view a few times. They all looked so calm. To them, this was routine, but to me, asking people if they had just murdered someone felt like I was entering the lion's den.

'Everything's ready on our end, Julie. You can start bringing them in one at a time. They're bound to have been talking to each other already, but that can't be helped. When we start the interviews, look for—' Jacqueline stopped talking and muted her microphone the moment Manu and Beau entered. Thibault's face was serious, but Manu was fidgeting.

My phone pinged with a text from Jacqueline. *Look for their mood or mental state. Check if they seem drunk or injured in any way. Give me an impression of their clothing: is it neat, wrinkled, stained (!), wet? And see if you can make out whether they're left or right-handed.*

That seemed doable. At least if I focussed on the details, my brain would have less opportunity to freak out. I showed the text to Thibault, who drew his sketchbook out of his back pocket and started making notes. I smiled at Manu in what I hoped was a calming manner. 'Tell me about him. Why did you invite him?'

I startled him with my question. It took him a second to realise I wasn't accusing him, but when he did, he relaxed the tiniest bit. He glanced at the video screen, where nobody seemed to be paying attention. 'For his influence, mostly. He wasn't an investor per se, like Corentin Bailly and Emile Lardy, but he had a say in many, many committees and organisations. I was hoping for his approval on a grant request to the Comité d'Histoire et du Patrimoine du Beaujolais. This is one of the oldest *domaines* in the region after all, and we do enough to preserve our heritage. I can't believe this happened.' Shaking his head, he rubbed his hand over his mouth, looking around the room at nothing in particular. Then he frowned. 'Benoît Le Roux is probably my best bet now.'

'The Mayor of Montmales? Why?'

'He's part of the committee as well. Not as well connected with the others, but for that particular grant I only need the approval of one committee member.'

'Carlier was here so you could butter him up?'

He pulled up one corner of his mouth in a crooked smile that didn't reach his eyes. 'I hope he at least enjoyed his last few hours.'

I snorted, then covered my mouth with my fingers. 'I'm sorry. But he didn't strike me as someone who enjoyed much of anything.'

Manu rubbed the back of his neck. 'You're right. The one thing he seemed to enjoy most was tearing apart whatever other people were enjoying at the time.'

Hm. Maybe that's why he hadn't said anything about Fabien's performance. In my eyes, there was plenty he could have said to raze the magician to the ground, but nobody else had been enjoying the show. 'Did he do it just to put people's hackles up?'

Pulling the corners of his mouth down and his eyebrows up, he answered, 'Who knows. Seems to have done.'

'So you didn't like him much.'

'Did anyone?'

Jacqueline tapped her mic, making us all jump.

'Good afternoon. I'm Capitaine Gavel. Since you're here, Monsieur Blanc-Mattieu, we'll start with you.'

Manu nodded. The way he sat in front of the screen, his great-great-some-more-greats grandfather would have been proud. Ramrod straight, no nerves showing any more, his expression fashionably bored, he awaited the first question.

While Jacqueline went through the introductory questions, I felt sorry for Manu. Instead of telling prospective investors about the wonderfulness of the place, he now had to answer questions about a murder. The rest of us only had to worry about staying alive, but he had the added uncertainty of the future of his business and his home.

'And where did you go after the show?' Jacqueline asked. I'd better start paying attention.

'I stayed in my office for a while, and then—'

'For how long?'

'Err... that must have been... about half an hour? Then I went outside to see if there was anything we could do about the bridge. When I came back, the staff informed me there had been a scream, so I went up to Monsieur Carlier's room, where I found the others.'

'Who was present there?'

Manu went through the rest of the story as I had already told it, without adding anything new. He'd gone straight to the conference room, where he'd been seen by staff and guests until Thibault announced that Julie had found the body.

'What was your relationship to the victim?'

'He was a representative of a committee I deal with on a professional basis.'

Jacqueline nodded. 'And what kind of man was he? Anything specific you can tell me that would help us identify who killed him?'

Though nothing else about him changed, Manu's fingers curled around the armrest. 'I'm afraid he wasn't very well liked. But I don't know of anything that would drive someone to kill him.'

When Jacqueline left a gap in the conversation, I took the opportunity. 'Did you recognise the murder weapon, the antler? Do you know where it came from?'

He shrugged in apology. 'There are so many of them scattered around the place... It could have come from anywhere. Sorry.'

Dead end number one. I wondered how many more we'd find.

Beau also felt he needed to add to the conversation and held up the handkerchief. 'Have you seen this before?'

Manu shook his head apologetically, and Jacqueline took over again. '*D'accord*, if there's nothing else you'd like to add, that will be all for now. Please provide Madame Belmain with a key to Monsieur Carlier's room. Thank you, Monsieur Blanc-Mattieu.'

Manu left, and Jacqueline turned to Beau and me. 'Impressions?'

I shrugged. 'I didn't see anything unnatural or special about him.'

'He was wearing a different shirt from this morning.'

Beau's sudden statement shocked me. Had I missed that? I stared at him open-mouthed, while I tried to remember what Manu had worn earlier. Dark blue, knitted something. Same as he'd had on just now? No! 'You're right! When he came in from the snow, his jumper had a yellow border around the neck. It was wet, and I kind of wondered why he hadn't buttoned up his coat in a snowstorm, but there was so much going on that I'd forgotten about that.' But Beau had noticed. I was impressed.

Jacqueline checked a notebook. 'From the list Thibault gave me, I think you should ask Madame la Vicomtesse in now.'

Thibault went out to fetch her, giving me some time to recover.

'Shocking, *hein?*' Jacqueline winked.

'Shut up.' I grinned back and shook my head. So I missed one thing. I know Beau had changed his shirt, too, but then he'd squashed chocolate between himself and Elise. She had changed her top even before lunch. People seemed to be changing shirts all over the place today.

The interview with Hélène Blanc-Mattieu went as expected. Her regal, calm presence seemed to influence even the police.

'I stayed behind after the show because I felt Monsieur Fabien needed to hear that he shouldn't drink so much before a performance.'

I bit my lip to keep from smiling. I could picture the scene – the vicomtesse with her quiet, caring voice telling overconfident Fabien exactly what he was doing wrong. From anyone else, he would have waved it away. But coming from her, it would have hit hard.

'We were still together when Madame Lardy screamed. I told Monsieur Fabien not to worry about it and rest for a while. When he'd retired, I joined the crowd outside Monsieur Carlier's room. From there, I took Madame Lardy to the kitchen for a cup of tea. I stayed with her for a few minutes, but she calmed down when Elise brought her cake.'

'Elise?'

'Elise Bonacieux, one of our staff.'

'Go on.'

'There's not much more. I went to my room to read. Madame Belmain came to fetch me for the presentation in the conference room, which I entered the moment Monsieur Fouquet got his text from Madame Belmain.'

'How well did you know Monsieur Carlier?'

'Not at all. I knew of him, since my son sometimes discusses business with me, but I only met him yesterday, when he arrived.'

Jacqueline looked straight into the camera. 'Is there anything else you can tell us? Even if it's just an impression?'

Madame Blanc-Mattieu ran her hand over her skirt, smoothing out an imaginary crease. But she hadn't noticed the stain yet or she would have changed. 'I'm sorry to say that I don't think he will be missed. He was an arrogant man with no regard for others. Of course, that is no reason for taking his life.' A slight frown underlined her words, but she offered no further insights.

'All right, thank you.'

The vicomtesse left, and Jacqueline once again posed the question, 'Impressions?'

Before I said anything, I glanced at Thibault. This time, he only shrugged.

'She's lovely,' I added. 'I can't imagine her having anything to do with killing a person.'

'And who would be capable, according to you?'

My cheeks heated. It felt like a mean question. How could I accuse anyone of murder at this point? Was it her way of asking me who I disliked? But maybe it was just her way of showing me I should not dismiss anyone if I wasn't ready to accuse another.

'To put it another way, who do you think we should ask in next?'

'Oh. Err...' Unfortunately, my first thought was, what would my choice say about me? My brain had some trouble suppressing my ego before I could answer the question logically. 'Probably Sandrine. She was sitting next to him at *déjeuner* and she found the body first.'

'Or at least, she screamed and brought all of our attention to it,' Beau said.

Right. Technically, nobody knew for certain that Carlier really had that antler sticking out of him at that point. But then, why would she scream and call it to anyone's attention if it hadn't happened yet? That made no sense. So technically, Beau was right, but now he was undermining me in front of the investigating officer. As soon as this was over, we had to have a serious talk.

My phone vibrated with another text. *Still haven't seen Maëline. She got lost. Keeps texting me she's fine and on her way, but I'm getting worried.*

David worried? This murder must be getting to him more than I'd thought. *She'll turn up. If she's texting, she's fine.* Probably. Now he had me questioning myself when I should be focussed on questioning others.

Sandrine was shaking violently when she came in, which didn't ease much when she sat down. Thibault put a glass of water on the table in front of her, but when she picked it up, the water splashed over the edge, and she put it down again.

'Please tell us your name and the reason you are in the Château de Montmales,' Jacqueline said after she'd introduced herself.

'Err... Sandrine Lardy. I... My husband was supposed to be here too, but he... couldn't. In the end. Work or... something.'

'Was it you or your husband who received the invitation?'

Sandrine kept her gaze firmly on the glass of water, which she clutched with both hands. 'My husband. He told me to go and... enjoy myself, even though he couldn't come. Because I'd been looking forward to it, you see.'

'I see. And were you? Enjoying yourself, I mean.'

Sandrine took her time to answer. Her voice was bitter when she did. 'Not really. I wanted Emile to be here. Even if he would only be here to see if he should invest. But he'd already decided, he said, so he didn't need to come and waste his time.'

'So was he going to invest or not?'

'I don't know.'

'And you were the one who first found the body of Marcel Carlier, is that correct?'

Sandrine whimpered, her knuckles white around the glass. Thibault couldn't help himself and crouched next to her, gently squeezing her shoulder.

'I was. I'd been in my room, checking social media to see if Emile had posted anything, but around three I got really bored. Marcel had told me at lunch that he considered his presence here a waste of time, too, especially now that the bridge was broken and there wouldn't be a party tomorrow. So I thought we might at least be bored together. I... knocked. He didn't answer. I called him, but he still didn't make a sound. He'd said he'd be in his room, so I got curious and looked through the keyhole. Then I... I saw him. He was...' Her voice broke on a sob.

I tried to stay detached. I knew she could be dramatic and I wanted to stay impartial, but the poor woman was a wreck. Beau did what he could, but she had some more crying to do before she could continue.

'I'm sorry,' she sniffled.

'It's all right. Perfectly understandable.' Jacqueline at her most magnanimous. She was not an emotional person and she did not have a lot of patience with emotional outbursts in others. Strangely, though, when she was doing her job, she could wait and wait until people were ready to talk. I'd learnt that myself when she was assigned to me after my ex-husband was arrested. Then when she'd become my friend, she shocked me with how little time she had for me when all I wanted to do was rant, without proposing a solution at the end. Right now, with Jacqueline in police mode, Sandrine would be given all the time she needed.

'He was' – Sandrine took a deep breath – 'on the floor. On a rug. But the rug was all stained. And then I saw the thing, the antler...' She swallowed. 'I scrambled back and screamed, then I ran away. I don't think I got very far, but I'm not sure. Madame Martin was there, she'll know where we were. I know she was trying to help, but she brought me right back to that awful place where... he... And then everyone else came, and they said they couldn't see anything, and when Monsieur Fouquet opened the door, he wasn't there! I thought I was going crazy! Until Madame Belmain went to fetch Madame Blanc-Mattieu, and he was back, and I was right, and he was dead.' She panted to fight more tears, whispering, 'I can't believe he's gone.'

'Did you know Monsieur Carlier before you came here?'

Sandrine nodded. 'Yes, he's on several committees that Emile deals with for work. He knows – knew – people in both the food industry and everything concerning local heritage. But he also had a finger in the pie of local small business ownership.'

'Would you have considered him a friend?'

That question brought some colour to Sandrine's cheeks. 'I... No, I don't think... He was... not an easy man to deal with. But he could be very understanding. He was going to talk – help me with... something. I don't know if he had any friends, really.'

'Can you think of anyone who might have wanted to harm him?'

She snorted, her distress momentarily swallowed by her habitual snobbery. 'Err... everyone? Well, not me, obviously. But he wasn't very popular. Because he was so well-connected, his colleagues feared excluding him more than they wanted to work with him. One word from Marcel to the wrong person, and your career could be in tatters. He'd done it before. Or, like with Jérémie Gümüs, failing to come to someone's aid could dent their reputation. Sometimes beyond repair.'

'What happened with Monsieur Gümüs?'

'Oh, I don't know all the details. But there was a rumour that his father had become rich by sweetening their wine with additives. Harmful additives. The wine was tested and proved absolutely fine, but Marcel wouldn't attest to their reputation because he said he couldn't guarantee it had always been good. Nearly cost Jérémie his business.'

15

I know you think I did it

'Seems like a good next candidate, this Jérémie,' Jacqueline said when Sandrine had left.

'That motive would have been better if his business had actually gone under, though.' Beau scrubbed his face with his hands.

I discreetly rubbed my eyes as well, taking care not to ruin my make-up. These conversations were tiring. Even though Beau and I didn't get to say or do much, we were constantly looking for clues and irregularities. At least, I assumed Beau was doing that too.

'Do you want tea or something?' Beau asked. 'I can get you one when I go get Jérémie.'

'That's a good idea,' Jacqueline butted in before I could answer. 'Have a short break. Don't forget you've had a shock today and you're not used to doing interviews.'

I shot Thibault a grateful smile.

'Tea?' he repeated.

'Yes, please.'

He left the room, and Jacqueline pounced. 'Marc is making me ask if you're sure you can trust Thibault. Of course, Marc doesn't trust you either, but we have to work with what we've got.'

I could see Marc Froment's disapproving face in the background. Jacqueline's partner had had to put up with me before and, even though things worked out well, he had never warmed to me. 'Thibault has absolutely nothing to do with this.'

Jacqueline hesitated. 'The thing is... as we see it now, there was a body in a locked room that disappeared and then reappeared. The most logical explanation is that someone has either a key or the skills to pick a lock. Right now, Thibault is the only one we know of who's in possession of one of those two things.'

'But we've only just started investigating.' I waved a dismissive hand. 'And the murderer isn't simply going to tell us he has the key. If that's what you're going after, Beau will be your primary suspect for a while. Except, he didn't know the victim and he was at my door a few seconds after Sandrine screamed. Hasn't left my sight since.'

Jacqueline gave a short nod. 'Good. That takes care of that.'

Thibault came in with two cups, followed by Jérémie Gümüs. The jittery man's gaze flitted from the screen to me and back. Though I'd been nervous through the first interviews, this was the first time I realised I'd be talking to the murderer in the course of the investigation. It might be Jérémie or it might be someone else, but what if they now saw me as a threat? Would that be enough motivation for them to kill me too? How afraid should I be? But before I could break into a fit of hyperventilation, a harsh, nasal voice sounded.

'Let's get this over with,' Jérémie said as he sat down. 'Wait, is this recorded? I don't want this recorded.'

'Monsieur Gümüs, thank you for joining us. My name is Capitaine Jacqueline Gavel, and this is my colleague Brigadier-chef Marc Froment. This is an official interview. Anything you say will be noted, whether we record or not.'

He crossed his legs, then uncrossed them and crossed them the other way. 'Is there a reward? For vital bits of information?'

'At this point, there is no reward, but may I remind you that you would be breaking the law should you withhold any evidence?'

Jérémie cleared his throat. 'I know you think I did it, but I didn't.'

'Why should we think you killed Marcel Carlier?'

Sneaky. *Give us your motive, Jérémie.* The man gave me the creeps, but I had to try and stay impartial. Still, one of these people was a murderer, and Jérémie had everything against him.

He seemed taken aback. 'Because he was a... he was always getting in my way. Everybody knew it, but they let him get away with it. For some reason. I *know* he had shady deals going on, but I could never prove it. Talk to Benoît Le Roux from the Comité d'Histoire et du Patrimoine du Beaujolais. He was not a fan either, but maybe he has some actual evidence.'

Jacqueline made a note, then continued, 'So what exactly was it Monsieur Carlier was getting in the way of?'

Jérémie wrinkled his nose, showing off his long, narrow teeth. 'My wine was rumoured to be tainted with sugar of lead. Adding anything to your wine, even water, can be considered an act of fraud, but adding poison to sweeten the wine would be a serious crime. Though, admittedly, my business was not doing as well as I'd hoped, I would never stoop so low as to corrupt my product.' Warming up to his subject, Jérémie turned a yellowish shade of pink, his eyebrows knitting together and his forehead showing little beads of sweat. His hands fisted on the table in front of him, he regained control of his tone before he continued. 'Even after extensive testing revealed no contamination of any kind, the damage had been done. My business is on the verge of bankruptcy. Naturally, I could never prove it, but I suspect the rumours originated with him.'

'Why do you think that?'

Inhaling through his nose, he cupped his hands, moving them up and down as if weighing his words. 'Because I wouldn't pay him.'

He said no more, and the silence lasted so long that I glanced at the screen to see if the connection had been lost. Jacqueline, however, was quietly waiting. Beau looked at me, too, probably wondering the same. What were we waiting for?

'Yes, I would have if I'd had the money! You have no idea how small this world is. One whiff of scandal and you're finished. That's why nobody ever spoke up, but I'm sure I wasn't the only one he approached. He was a one-man Mafia.'

'I see.' Jacqueline scribbled something on a piece of paper out of sight of the camera.

'Do you? I had every reason to hate him, but if I were going to kill him, I should have done it months earlier. He'd already done his worst to me.'

'Where were you at the time of the murder?'

'In my room. Alone. I'll go lock myself in there, shall I?' Leaning back in his chair, he crossed his arms over his chest.

'We are not accusing anyone at this time, Monsieur Gümüs. Thank you. That will be all for now. Please keep yourself available to Madame Belmain for further investigation.'

Jérémie threw me a distrusting look but then left, and I stretched my arms out above me to relieve my sore muscles and hide an unprofessional shudder. 'He's very quick to accuse himself.'

'In hopes that we won't, obviously.' Beau drained his cup and slid it onto the table.

'But it did confirm what Madame Lardy said.' Jacqueline pursed her lips. 'It looks like Monsieur Carlier had plenty of enemies. So which one are we going to talk to next?' She switched off her microphone to talk to Marc and another person, whose hands alone were just visible in the frame. 'Thibault, bring in Benoît Le Roux, please.'

He saluted and left, taking our empty cups with him.

'I'm sorry to keep going like this, Julie, but the sooner we establish a complete picture, the better.'

'I understand.' I did. But I also got up to stretch my legs. I'd been in this room for over an hour, trying to catch the slightest incongruence. So far, everyone seemed to be telling the truth. The mayor of Montmales was up next. Had he been blackmailed too? Sometimes I wondered how my mother dealt with all these types.

'Madame Belmain.' The booming baritone of Benoît Le Roux always seemed to precede him – as if he violated the scientific facts about the relative speeds of sound and light. I'd only met him on one or two occasions before today, but he was impossible to ignore. 'How is your mother?'

If my mother was to be believed, the mayor of Montmales had a soft spot for her. He had befriended her on several social media platforms and sent her private messages when he found an article on antiques or books that he thought she'd enjoy. 'She is quite well, thank you.'

'Good, good. I'm glad. Dreadful business, this.' He said it as if talking about the snowstorm. An inconvenience, but nothing more. His introduction to the police was almost jolly.

'And you were invited in your official capacity as mayor?'

'Yes and no. While I am the mayor of Montmales, in this case the main reason for my invitation was my involvement in the Comité d'Histoire et du Patrimoine du Beaujolais. The Comité gives out several grants a year, one of which I suspect the vicomte is hoping to secure.'

'What are his chances, do you know?'

Benoît Le Roux raised his eyebrows. 'He is certainly a contender, but whether or not his chances have improved with the death of Marcel Carlier, I cannot say. We'll need to appoint a new member to be able to vote on this.'

'The Comité is also how you knew Monsieur Carlier?'

A cloud passed over Benoît's face. 'Mostly, yes. I had been in contact with him through other channels but had not worked beside him until I was elected into the Comité.'

'How was he, to work with?'

He remained silent for a beat. Then he cleared his throat. 'Not speaking ill of the dead is going to be very difficult in his case. I honestly cannot think of a decent thing I've seen him do in the short time we worked together.'

'He joined the Comité later?'

'Oh no, he'd been there forever. It was I who had only been elected two or maybe two and a half months ago.'

'Can you elaborate on his and your tasks within the Comité?'

Benoît sat up straight. Oh, he was ready to elaborate. The jolly smile was back in place, and his hands zoomed back and forth to underline his words. 'In effect, we had the same role. Members of the Comité are contacted by individuals and organisations that contribute to keeping alive the history and heritage of the Beaujolais region. The Comité then visits the sites and decides whether or not they have done enough to be a contender. In the case of this château, for example, the vicomte is responsible for the upkeep of a 750-year-old building. That alone requires a small fortune. But apart from the obvious contribution to the history of the region, he has also made the *vendanges*, picking the grapes at the end of summer, into an experience people pay to have. True, the yield per person is not as great as you'd have with paid workers, but you've got to admit, it's pretty clever. Besides the financial advantage, of course, it advertises the Beaujolais way of life as an adventure, a positive event in the minds of tourists and wine consumers. That, to me, is worthy of a grant.'

'And did Monsieur Carlier share that opinion?'

'He never shared his feelings on any project until the very end. If you ask me, he enjoyed leaving prospective contenders in limbo, seeing them sweat with insecurity.'

'Was there ever anything... untoward in his behaviour?'

He narrowed his eyes at the screen; Jacqueline's face was inscrutable. 'I have nothing substantial to give you on that subject, and I'd rather not resort to gossip. I have a feeling that's what you already have.'

Huh. Look at old Benoît being all incorruptible. Not as silly as he looked, that one.

'All right. Where were you at the time the murder took place?'

'I was in my room.'

'Can anyone confirm that?'

Benoît's moustache twitched. 'Perhaps. One of the staff brought me a cup of coffee. I think her name is Elise.'

'That is all for now, *Monsieur le Maire*. Thank you.'

'Not at all. Anything I can do...'

He sailed out of the room, which seemed to expand as soon as he'd left. He was a character all right, but was he a murderer? The more people I didn't suspect, the more I was left with a general feeling of suspicion towards all of them.

'Elise now?' Thibault hitched his thumb over his shoulder.

'Yes, please. He seemed eager to get her,' she added to me after Beau had left.

'Oh, you caught that, huh? I don't know how he always finds them so quickly.'

Jacqueline flashed me a crooked smile that disappeared before any of her colleagues could pick it up. 'So he did not know this girl before he came to the château?'

'Not as far as I know, but by all means ask him.'

'Don't worry, I will. Probably best if we take a little break after this interview. How many more do we have?' She counted on a list. 'One, two... five? Yes, best to take a break, see what we've got so far. Ah, you must be Elise?'

'Elise Bonacieux.' She nodded as she sat down, wriggling a few times before clamping her hands together on the table before her.

'Your name has come up a few times already.' Jacqueline said it with a smile before introducing herself, but Elise didn't seem to pick up on that. Her knuckles turned white. Why was she so jittery? From what I'd seen, she'd been doing her job very well – apart maybe from that little indiscretion with Beau earlier, but would that make her nervous?

'How well did you know the victim, Marcel Carlier?'

'Not at all, really. Just met him yesterday. He blamed me for coffee he spilled on himself, but he wasn't the first and he won't be the last.'

'So you didn't like him much?'

Elise wrung her hands, taking a quick breath. 'I didn't really think about him at all. He was just one of the guests. Maybe he stood out a bit in a negative way, but not more so than other clients we've had.'

'Do you often have guests in the château?'

Her eyes widened. 'Oh, I didn't mean here. I'm with a company that caters and provides staff for big events. We come here every so often for weddings and parties, but it's not our only venue. I've seen mothers-of-the-bride much worse than him.'

'Where were you at the time of the murder?'

'I...' She was sweating now. 'I'm not sure. I know I brought Monsieur Le Roux something, a drink, at some point. Water? Maybe?'

Jacqueline didn't react, but Beau looked up.

'Or was it coffee? I can't remember.' She let out a nervous giggle, mostly aimed at Beau.

'All right. Thank you, Madame Bonacieux.'

Elise's shoulders immediately relaxed, but her wide, relieved smile froze when Jacqueline asked, 'Excuse me, one last question, if I may. Did you bring him anything else?'

'No!' She said it far too quickly to be believable, but Jacqueline let it pass.

Thibault brought Elise back to the kitchen, and I turned to Jacqueline.

'What's with the Columbo move?'

'Tell me, what's the atmosphere like?'

Okay, so she wasn't going to tell me. 'You mean before the murder, or now?'

'Both.'

I shrugged. 'You know I never fit in at events like these. None of them seem to like each other very much, but maybe that's normal. And ever since I found the body' – I shivered at the recollection – 'I've been trying to help you, so I don't know what they're all doing. Except for Maëline, who's apparently lost in the castle somewhere.'

Jacqueline frowned. 'Take a break. Try and find Maëline. If you could send the vicomte in here, then we can deal with some of the staff without you. We'll try to rule out as many of them who were together, so you don't have to be present at every single interview.'

I nodded with a yawn. '*Merci*. I'll go stretch my legs and see what people are up to. Message me when you know who you want to see next.'

Though I was happy to leave the conference room, I was in no hurry to join the others. Like I'd told Jacqueline, I didn't fit in with this crowd. Yes, I was used to that, but I wasn't in the habit of accusing the people I didn't fit in with. Not that I was personally accusing them, but I doubt they would see it that way. I was working with the police, so I was above suspicion, but not to them. To them, I was the spy, the mole, maybe even the double agent. Beau would love that idea. Me, not so much.

I frowned. The last two days had sucked. First David had an accident. Then I got a bunch of snow on my head. Then I nearly got run over. Then I had to come to this party of posh people. Then a toad got murdered. And finally, everyone was going to hate me for thinking I'd accuse them of said murder. An impossible murder at that! Because while everyone seemed to have some sort of motive, nobody had the opportunity, as far as I could tell. I wondered if Jacqueline had worked out the timeline of the disappearing body yet.

When I eventually found my way to the *petit salon*, all eyes cut to me expectantly.

'Has Jérémie confessed?' asked Sandrine Lardy.

Along with Thibault and Elise – and of course Maëline – only Jérémie Gümüs was missing. He must have gone back to his room, thinking everyone would only accuse him. Looks like he was right.

'No one has confessed. Monsieur Blanc-Mattieu, the capitaine would like you to arrange for the staff to see her.'

Manu gave a short nod and left, but all the others kept staring at me.

'So?' said Corentin Bailly. 'Any news?'

'They're still working on it.'

'And what are we supposed to do in the meantime?' asked Sandrine. 'Sit here and wait to be killed?'

Benoît Le Roux answered that at a relatively civilised volume. 'As long as we're all together, the killer can't get to us.'

'And what about tonight? When we all go our separate ways?'

'What motive would the killer have to murder you?' Corentin asked, leaving Sandrine unable to answer that impossible question.

Hélène Blanc-Mattieu sighed. 'What motive does anyone have to take another person's life?'

'I can think of a few things,' mumbled Romy Martin, the journalist.

Right at that moment, my phone pinged. *Bring in Romy Martin.*

16

That glance was not a friendly one

'Madame Martin, you are a reporter?'

'Yes, I write for *Le Courant*.' Romy sat up straight on her chair, her hands folded loosely on the table.

'I take it you were aware of Monsieur Carlier's position in the community before you came to Château de Montmales?'

'I was.'

'Did you know him personally?'

Romy thought about that. 'Not... personally, no. I had had some correspondence with him, but I wouldn't call that "knowing him personally".'

'What was your correspondence about?'

She pressed her lips together before she answered. 'I wanted to interview him for an article, but he was reluctant to accommodate me.'

'Did you ask him again when you saw him there?'

'I did.'

'And?'

'He brushed me off, not promising either yes or no, but "not now".' Nothing in Romy's attitude said she'd expected any other response.

'Where were you when he was killed?'

'On a call to my editor.'

Did that sound rehearsed? If it was, that might not mean anything. The question was to be expected, so the guests would have thought of their answer beforehand. Perhaps Elise had been nervous because she couldn't think of the exact thing she'd been doing at the time. Romy showed no nerves at all.

'And you were the first to encounter Madame Lardy after she screamed?'

'That's right. The corridor she was in runs up to the landing where I was, so I met her halfway.'

'Does that mean you had the door to Monsieur Carlier's room within view the whole time?'

'Within seconds, yes.'

'And no one came in or out?'

'Obviously, or I would have mentioned it.'

Jacqueline stared at her desk a few seconds. It wasn't hard to figure out why. If the window of opportunity to hide the body while Sandrine was away wasn't bigger than a few seconds, then how had the body disappeared?

'Can you think of anything else you might have picked up during your stay here that would help us in our investigation?'

My ears perked up. Up till now, Jacqueline had added the sentence mostly as a standard reminder at the end of the interview. Why did she turn it into a question for the journalist? I kept a sharp eye on Romy to see if it made her feel differently. All she did, though, was narrow her eyes.

'Not directly related. I could, of course, use my investigative skills, but...' She glanced at me. I don't think she meant to, because she redirected her gaze at the screen and kept it there for the rest of the interview. I had the feeling, though, that the glance was not a friendly one, and it unsettled me. 'I understand that you don't want any information leaked, but I am a reporter, and a murder in an isolated *domaine* is a pretty big scoop. I won't sit on it forever. The public—'

'Deserves to know, yes. We know. Please, do give us some time to do our job, Madame Martin. It couldn't hurt your scoop if you can add that you yourself have helped the police catch a killer.'

At that, Romy's eyes lit up. Jacqueline certainly knew her customers.

'We'll let you know as soon as we're ready to release information to the public. Thank you, Madame Martin.'

Romy remained seated. 'You might want to check out Corentin Bailly...'

'Why is that?'

'Of all the people here today, he had the strongest link to the deceased. They were regularly in contact over all kinds of issues, both for business and politics.'

'Are you aware of any ill feelings between the two?'

'No... not as such. But anyone dealing with Marcel Carlier for that amount of time is bound to have a grudge somewhere. I'm sorry if this isn't a very professional thing to say, because I've never been able to prove it, but it's very likely that he was into some shady deals. Again, I'd be happy to do some digging if I can depend on a heads-up in return.'

'And again, we will let you know. Thank you.'

She made her way out quite reluctantly, throwing me another of those hostile looks over her shoulder.

I cut Jacqueline off before she could say it. 'Impressions? I can tell you right now that she doesn't like me. I didn't catch that before, but I think she suspects me of getting in the way of her scoop.'

'I for one think she was lying about where she was,' Thibault added. 'Her room is in a completely different part of the castle, so why would she be on a call to her editor on a landing close to Carlier's room?'

'How do you know that? About her room?' Jacqueline asked.

'Elise told me. Well, she said she had to go clean up something Romy had spilled, and she grumbled about all the stairs. Carlier's tower room is only one flight up.'

'Do you think she'd be ruthless enough to kill for a story?' I asked him, but he only shrugged. Did *I* think she'd kill for a story? What if she had? I tried to puzzle together how that would work, but Jacqueline broke my concentration.

'Can you bring in Corentin Bailly, Beau? It's getting late, but I'd like to see all the guests before dinner. We'll do the staff afterwards, as they all have alibis provided by at least one other staff member. The guests all have better motives too.'

'There's only Corentin and Apolline left,' I said as Beau went to fetch Corentin.

'Any thoughts on them?'

'Well, as much as I'd like to suspect Apolline, she and her husband came running from the opposite direction after Sandrine screamed, so even if either of them had killed Carlier earlier, I don't see how they could have hidden him and then put him back.'

'You're right. Theoretically, most of the guests would have had the opportunity to kill Monsieur Carlier before the scream. But afterwards, most of them were with others most of the time. We'll have to be very precise in our chronology. *Bonsoir*, Monsieur Bailly.'

I turned, and for one fraction of a second, Corentin reminded me of Marcel Carlier. He was younger, but of the same height and build. His hair had less grey in it, but because it was a little lighter, the overall hue came close to that of the dead man. He even wore the same expression of bored arrogance. The similarities made me shiver, but I shook off the unease with a deep breath.

Jacqueline had gone through her introductions and was now questioning Corentin on his relationship to Carlier.

'We had had some dealings together in the past, and he now regularly advised me on business decisions.'

'Did you pay him for his... advice?'

Both his right eye and his lips twitched, but the movement was very subtle. 'I may have offered him discounts or compensation, but those were more gestures of friendship or appreciation than direct payment.'

'I see. Would you have considered him a friend?'

He hesitated. In my eyes, that said enough. 'We didn't share more than a professional relationship, but we did see each other quite often.'

I had the feeling Jacqueline was looking at me on her screen. We would probably have shared a look if she were here. Then again, if she were here, I probably wouldn't have been.

'Where did you go after lunch?'

'We – that is, my wife and I – went to our room for a little *sieste*, where we stayed until Madame Lardy startled us. We arrived at Marcel's door at the same time as Madame Belmain.' He gestured to me.

I nodded, and Jacqueline thanked him.

'Can you think of anyone who could have done this?'

Corentin snorted. 'Isn't that *your* job? From what I know, it could be anyone, even that ridiculous magician. To be honest, the man didn't interest me too much when he was alive and he interests me even less now that he is dead. But for one brief moment, he will make a story, and who knows what some people will do for a story.'

It was such a vague accusation, Jacqueline didn't even ask him if he could back it up. Still, that was the second time my suspicions were drawn towards Romy Martin.

'Madame Belmain has been charged with the investigation on site, so please direct any concerns towards her and keep yourself available in case she has any more questions.'

Corentin tilted his head back even further when he looked at me, his disdain obvious. 'I suppose you know what you're doing, Capitaine. I, for my part, will do whatever it takes to uphold the good name of the Beaujolais.'

Even if that meant dealing with me, apparently.

Thibault escorted Corentin out, and I made a face at Jacqueline. 'So, why haven't you found the killer yet? Corentin's waiting, you know.'

'Maybe he should pay me off too.'

I laughed, imagining Jacqueline as corrupt. Those two didn't match at all. 'How would that work? You'd pick a random suspect and arrest them?'

'Sure, why not?' She grinned. 'Any preferences?'

'His wife, maybe?'

Speaking of... Apolline blew into the room with a flourish. She looked like she was enjoying her moment in the spotlight more than anything, waving her arms about as if her audience was in the back of the theatre instead of on the other end of a video call.

'Julie, *ma chère*, what an awful happenstance. How fortunate we are to have you here.'

Oh! I'd gone up in the world. My connections must be worth more than my 'little business'.

'Madame Bailly, I'm Capitaine Jacqueline Gavel—'

'*Enchantée.*'

'Can you tell us, what was your relationship with the deceased like?'

'That poor man. I can't imagine why anyone would want to murder him. He was always helping us out with various things, so he probably did that for others as well. I find it unbelievable that someone would want to, you know... get rid of him.'

'So you are not aware of any bitterness towards him?'

'Oh, no. I mean, sure, he should have let us have that membership to the ABGC, but—'

'The ABGC?' Beau asked.

She pulled up an eyebrow, as if she'd only just realised Thibault was in the room. Her nose rose slightly when she explained, 'The Association Beaujolais Grand Cru. It's a prestigious organisation most people would kill to be part of.' She paled when she realised what she'd said. 'Not that we did! Or would. Obviously. I'm sorry, I shouldn't have said that.'

'But you are not members?'

'No. Marcel was trying to get us in – it's by invitation only, you see – but he said we were denied access.'

'You think he wasn't telling the truth?'

'Well... I have no proof of this, so keep that in mind' – that was becoming the phrase of the day – 'but I think he never asked. I meant to confront him on the matter but hadn't found the right moment to do so yet. Now I suppose I never will. *Tiens.*' She waved her hand in defeat. 'So, what we need to do now is find out who was where after lunch. Then we should find out who had these hidden hostile feelings towards poor Marcel. Do you think you can do that, Capitaine Gavel?'

'Our training usually helps us quite well in dealing with this kind of situation, Madame Bailly.'

Apolline scoffed, 'Ah, but this situation is quite different, wouldn't you say? I should think you don't deal with persons of interest of this calibre daily. You should be thankful you have Madame Belmain here to aid you. She at least knows some more of the goings-on at this level of society.'

Gee, thanks for the recommendation.

'We will be sure to ask Madame Belmain for her insight during our investigation. Is there anything else you would like to add that may be of use?'

'You should talk to that server girl, that Elise. I know you already did, but did you find out she had a spot of bother with Marcel this morning? She emptied a cup of coffee all over his jacket. Out of spite, I'm sure. Jealous people will do anything, mark my words.'

'Thank you, Madame Bailly, you may go.'

'Yes, please go,' I added, pushing the door closed behind her. 'Can you believe my mother makes me sit through hours of meetings with her each month?'

'At least we have you to guide us through her world of unimaginable glory.' She made a sideways eye roll at someone off-screen. 'Marc has reminded me that that remark was not very professional. Please accept my apology.'

I grinned.

'Any more customers?' Beau asked when he returned. 'I asked everyone about that handkerchief as I brought them here, but nobody showed any signs of recognition, so that's another dead end. Fabien le Fabuleux's handkerchiefs we've seen, and they're quite different, but he seemed keen to be interviewed.'

'I think we should let you have some dinner first.' She nodded at a colleague. 'We need to go through all this information. Please keep your phone charged at all times and don't get murdered.'

'Sound advice. I intend to keep it. Talk to you later.' I broke the connection, looked at Thibault, and let my shoulders droop. 'Now what?'

'Food,' he stated.

Probably best. I don't know what I'd expected to gain from these interviews, but not knowing any more than this morning wasn't it. Plenty of motive, no opportunity. On the one hand, the fact that Carlier's murderer probably had a good motive was somewhat comforting. But since we still had no idea who it was, in theory any one of us could still be a target. I stayed close to Beau all the way to the dining room. Maybe the others had recovered from the shock enough for some idle chitchat over dinner. Who knows what that might reveal.

17

Where have you been?

Finally, the dining room! This castle was far too big for Maëline to be wandering by herself. There were corridors she knew she'd passed at least six times. Unless they had reproductions of the same medieval painting of two people playing chess in six different places. And that was only the second time she got lost. After that odd screaming sound, she'd found her way to the kitchen and back with the help of Sacha's map, but when she'd tried to find her room, the castle had decided to change itself, and it had taken her half an hour to locate it.

There, she'd composed an email to her boss telling him to find her a new client, but she'd held off on tapping *Send*. She'd reread it later to make sure it wasn't whiny or unprofessional. Also, if she left David, she'd be back to square one, sleeping on her friend's couch. Maybe if she could get him to apologise, she might not have to find a new place to stay? But then, apologies seemed far from his mind. To David's increasingly haughty texts demanding she join him, she replied with a *Sorry, still lost*. She doubted he believed her, but it gave her a little time to regain her calm and make a plan.

She *could* go back to her friend's couch for a couple of days until her boss found her a new client. And if she didn't have to work for David any more, she didn't have to pretend to be nice in the meantime. If he didn't want her here, she didn't want to be here. On the other hand, they were still trapped in this château for probably at least another day, so to avoid an outburst, spending as little time as possible in David's presence was key.

After a while, she expected it wouldn't be long until dinner, so she'd ventured outside her room and promptly got lost again. She should ask Manu for a floorplan. Eventually, she did make it to the dining room, where she was attacked before her other foot had made it over the threshold.

'There you are! We haven't seen you in over four hours. Where have you been?'

Why did everything David said sound like an accusation? 'I got lost. I told you that.'

Instead of claiming their seats at the long table, people had scattered around the dining room. Without the usual chatter, it was eerily quiet. David, as well, did not look his usual self. His hair was mussed and there were dark circles under his eyes. He looked... worried?

'Don't you realise how suspicious that looks?' he asked.

So much drama. Was it only yesterday morning that she'd thought he was attractive? 'Nobody even knows me. Why would it be suspicious if I wasn't in sight.' She didn't bother to make it sound like a question. Who would care where she was? She wasn't supposed to be here in the first place. David had said so himself. If it weren't for finding Sacha, she might have believed him by now.

'Everyone is going to think you had something to do with the murder.'

She stared at him. 'What murder? Have you started a mystery game or something?'

It was his turn to stare. 'Marcel Carlier was murdered this afternoon. Didn't you hear the scream? Julie has been working with the police to interview everyone. And you have been walking around alone. Unprotected. Who knows what could have happened. Those texts could have been sent by anyone with your phone. Next time you get lost for four hours, please, just answer your calls.'

Maëline sat down slowly. Then she glanced around the room. 'Someone here murdered Monsieur Carlier?'

David's dark look softened slightly. 'At least they were all here. So unless there's someone in the château we don't know about, you were fairly safe.'

But there was! Maëline bit her lip. No, that didn't matter. She herself had been with Sacha when they heard the scream.

So Sacha couldn't be the murderer, and Maëline didn't have to tell on her.

She was still processing this new information when the vicomtesse rose and addressed the room. '*Mesdames et messieurs*, words cannot describe how I feel on this sad occasion. There was supposed to be a celebration. Instead, we are all wondering who amongst us could have performed such an atrocious deed. But let me...' She gave a short sigh. 'Let me offer you some controversial consolation. Though Monsieur Carlier was an odious man, the police are doing their utmost to find the killer. But *because* he was an odious man, I venture to say that the rest of us should be safe. Whatever the reason was for killing Monsieur Carlier, that reason probably doesn't apply to the rest of us.' She paused for another breath. 'Whether or not you will allow yourself to be comforted by that thought, please come to the table together. Let's try to enjoy the meal that our chef has worked so hard for.'

Nobody moved. Only Manu and his mother were already at the table, but the others stayed where they were. David was the first to push himself up and hobble to the long table. Maëline hurried after him. The news of a murder still had her a bit stunned, but she would show Manu and Hélène support in any way she could. Fabien the magician, who had been sitting by himself, was next, followed by Benoît Le Roux.

The others were left staring at each other from across tables. Corentin got up and took his wife by the elbow. Sandrine clamped her eyes shut, her knuckles white around a glass of water, then joined the others at the big table. Julie and Thibault came in at that moment and naturally joined everyone. Only Jérémie was now left sitting by himself.

'Monsieur Gümüs?' Hélène Blanc-Mattieu asked.

'I don't trust the lot of you. Any one of you could have killed him. None of you are too fond of me. Who's to say this won't be my last meal?'

'Then at least eat your last meal. We are all here and can't kill you while you're eating.'

'Yeah? Unless they use poison.'

Right at that moment the soup was served and the whole sequence repeated itself. Everyone stared at their plates, wondering if it would be safe to eat, until Manu, Hélène, and David picked up their spoons and started eating.

Maëline should be next. There wasn't really any reason to suspect the soup. Nobody knew her, so why would they kill her? And it looked delicious. After walking around for hours, she was starving. The others seemed to be fine. She might as well try one bite.

But after one bite she was sold. The soup was as tasty as it looked and her stomach was screaming for more. By the time she'd emptied her plate, all the others were eating too. When the servers took the plates away, David struck up a conversation with Manu, and after the main course, everyone was talking. Everyone except Jérémie Gümüs, who remained at a table by himself, arms crossed and frowning.

Fabien had been talking to Maëline about his travels. Though she didn't believe a word he said (were there still maharajahs lying on cushions in palaces filled with dancing maidens?), she was grateful for the distraction. Julie had moved to what would have been Jérémie's seat and was gesticulating in her conversation with Romy Martin and the vicomtesse. Across the table from Maëline, Apolline was talking to the mayor of Montmales, while Beau followed her words with a curious expression on his face. There was fascination, but also a kind of abhorrence. With no small amount of amusement mixed in.

Maëline felt a pang of jealousy for the way in which Thibault seemed to breeze through life. She'd only taken this job to have a roof over her head and now she was locked in a castle with a murderer, wondering if it wouldn't have been better if she'd stayed on her friend's couch. But *he* didn't seem to have a care in the world. *I'm locked in a castle with a murderer, so what?*

'Don't you think?'

Uh-oh. Now she was supposed to answer an unknown question. Time to pull out the non-committal grunt, something the French language is exceptionally well suited for, fortunately. Fabien accepted it without a second thought. He continued his story about... crayfish? How had he got to there from maharajahs?

Desert was a peppermint ice cream that had everyone silent for a few minutes. Now that their faces were at rest, they showed the toll of the day's events. All of them, including Thibault, Maëline noticed with a delight that made her feel guilty, looked tired. Cheeks were paler, wrinkles seemed deeper, and Julie, along with some others, sported bags under her eyes.

'No, not at all,' Sandrine suddenly said, louder than she'd probably intended.

Corentin, who was sitting next to her and had asked the question to which that had been an answer, grinned apologetically across the table at Maëline.

'No, if he can open them that easily' – she pointed her thumb at Thibault on her other side – 'those locks don't make me feel safe at all. I wish Emile was here. How am I supposed to sleep in a room all by myself?' She teared up and took a handkerchief out of her purse that was already smeared liberally with mascara stains.

Thibault had turned to her and placed a hand on her shoulder, but she shook it off. He looked perplexed. Typical.

'Madame Lardy,' Maëline began, but she was cut off by Romy Martin.

'I agree. I for one don't feel safe either. Perhaps we should all sleep here.'

'I'm not doing that.' That was Corentin Bailly. 'It'll just bring me closer to the killer. I'm staying in my comfortable bed in my comfortable room.'

Several other people nodded. Jérémie Gümüs grumbled, 'So what if I get killed? Nothing to live for now.'

'Montmales. More like Mont Malaise,' Sandrine wailed. 'Mount Misery, that's what it is.'

'You're welcome to share my room, Sandrine, if you trust me.'

Sandrine gave Romy a once-over, then accepted her offer, and the two women and Manu excused themselves to make the necessary arrangements.

Julie scooted over to the chair next to Maëline. 'How about you? Will you feel safe enough?'

Maëline shrugged. 'Who would want to kill me? None of these people know me, and I haven't seen anything I shouldn't have.' Well, nothing related to the murder, anyway. Sacha was in a completely different part of the château when Sandrine screamed. She glanced around and lowered her voice. 'It's strange to think that one of these people has taken a life, though. Do you think they meant to? Because if it was an accident, maybe there's less chance of them doing it again.'

'You don't stab someone in the back with an antique antler by accident.'

Maëline wrinkled her nose. 'No, I don't suppose you do. Do you think it was planned, though?'

'Difficult to say. Would you plan to kill someone with an antler? Seems more like a weapon of convenience to me. On the other hand, I looked for a nail or a hook when I was taking pictures in the room, but there didn't seem to be any place the antler could have hung, so that would suggest the killer did bring it to the room. So perhaps they planned it, but not long enough in advance to take a good weapon? Manu didn't know where the antler came from either. It's so frustrating. And worrying, to say the least.'

She got up to offer her chair to her brother, who'd joined them. Thibault leaned over the table to pitch in. 'I don't think any of us need to be scared. We're all nice people. He wasn't.'

David nodded slowly. 'He seemed to have given plenty of people cause to hate him. When you were conducting the interviews, all anyone could talk about is how they weren't surprised it was him that got killed.'

Beau held his palm up over the table. 'But Sandrine and Romy are still afraid they'll be murdered too. What does that say about them?'

'Don't you think that's normal?' asked Maëline. 'A man has been murdered. Isn't it a logical reaction to be afraid?'

'Not if the person killed was Tweedy Toad.'

'Julie!'

Julie's cheeks turned slightly pink, but she didn't seem too remorseful at her lack of respect. In a way, Maëline could understand. When her own father passed away, her first thought had been 'good riddance'. Maybe her guilt about that was why she was now more sensitive on the subject.

'If you're concerned, Maëline, you can always unlock the door between our rooms.'

Maëline blinked at David. He probably meant nothing untoward, but...

Julie snorted. 'What good would that do? You can't even walk. You're better off unlocking the door between our rooms.'

David looked up and down the little, plump figure of his big sister, not concealing any contempt for her abilities as a knight in shining armour.

'Oh, just unlock all the doors, and I will rescue each and every one of you,' Beau announced, his arms wide. Everyone chuckled, though none of them seemed to find it very funny.

Maëline's thoughts drifted to Sacha, alone and cold in her abandoned wing. Maëline had managed to take her a nice stash of food, but Sacha would soon run out again if Maëline couldn't find an excuse to sneak off. And if they had to wait for the snowstorm to settle before the bridge could be repaired, they'd have to spend all of tomorrow together as well. Would it even be a good idea to try and visit Sacha with a killer on the loose?

'But how can that be? Everyone was somewhere else at the time of the murder,' Thibault was saying.

'Obviously, sweet boy, someone is lying. Question is, who is it?'

He turned to Julie and narrowed his eyes. 'If you ask me, it's Jérémie Gümüs. The whole "it's obvious that everyone must think I killed Marcel" is a double bluff, and he actually did do it.'

'But he came running with Benoît Le Roux while we were there, so he couldn't have been inside at the time.'

'You think the killer was in there while you were all standing outside?' David asked.

'I don't see how else the body could have disappeared after Sandrine's scream. The door was unguarded for no more than a few seconds.'

'Unless the killer ran the other way, then turned around when he saw Benoît, and pretended to have come running from another direction.' Beau apparently still thought it was Jérémie.

'Then where did he hide the body?'

'Sandrine could have been lying. If the murder took place after she screamed...' David looked like he was still working on the next bit of that sentence when Julie voiced the problem with that idea.

'Why would she do that? No, I think our best bet is to find out who had the best— Oh, that's Jacqueline, I'd better take this.'

She motioned for Beau to follow her, leaving Maëline with David.

'Maëline...'

Could she make an excuse? Talking to him alone wasn't very high on her list at the moment.

'I'm... sorry?'

Oh, this could be interesting. 'You're not sure?'

'I'm not sure it's enough. I've been a bit... prickly. I'm not used to having to depend on other people, and with this whole thing of coming to the château, and then the murder...'

Excuses, excuses.

'What I mean is, I'm sorry I was rude to you earlier.'

That looked painful. Maëline was about to accept his apology when Manu strode in. David visibly stiffened.

'Hey, you two! You're the last ones here. Everyone else has gone up to their rooms. Would you like to join me in the *petit salon*, so the staff can clear the table?'

David winced. 'No, I think I'll go up as well. Maëline, would you...?'

'Oh, don't bother her. Here, I'll help you. What are friends for, *quoi*? If you break yourself, I'll pick up the pieces.'

He moved to pick David up around his waist, but David jumped back surprisingly quickly on one foot. 'No, thanks. I don't need *your* help.'

Was that emphasis only in Maëline's head?

Manu didn't seem to have picked up on it. 'All right. Then do you mind if Maëline joins me for hot chocolate in the salon? I mean, if you...?' He raised his eyebrows at Maëline, who looked at David.

'I think she's old enough to make her own decisions.' David paused, then when Maëline nodded at Manu, he mumbled, 'Whether they're wise ones...'

So much for apologising for being rude. Manu threw his friend a curious look, then held out his elbow, which Maëline took. He steered her around David with a cheery 'Good night, then.'

What had she done to make David so sour? Or was he always like this, and had yesterday morning been an exception?

With her thoughts revolving around David's mood and Sacha's need, Maëline didn't have much attention left for Manu. She kept having to ask him to repeat what he'd said or asked, but Manu was a gracious host and after half an hour of stumbling conversation, he suggested she get some sleep. That was probably best. Maëline got up but froze when the wind howled around a corner of the ancient château.

'Don't worry about it. That's just great-great uncle Mattís, still chasing chambermaids.'

Maëline giggled. 'You must have grown up with very different bedtime stories than the rest of us.'

He smiled. 'A place with so much history will always have less pleasant stories to tell. I'm only sorry you have to be mixed up in one of them. Uncle Mattís isn't actually the worst of them. You want to hear about La Dame Blanche de Montmales?'

'Who's she?'

'The first wife of one of my ancestors, Louis the Fat. She was beautiful. Pale skin, dark hair, big brown eyes. She caught the attention of one of the Sires de Beaujeu, who tried to lead her astray when Louis was away. But she was a keen chess player and agreed to sleep with him if he could win a game. She beat him, so he killed her.'

Maëline gasped.

'She's said to haunt a part of the château we don't use now. She's been seen by several people. Unfortunately, she died childless. Louis's second wife, the one who gave him heirs, was mostly known for being the same size as her husband...'

'What was her name? The White Lady, I mean.'

'Sara. She was Spanish, actually. Came from... Cordoba? I'm not sure now.'

'Toledo?'

He raised his eyebrows. 'I think you're right. How did you know that?'

'I didn't.' It was all probably just an eerie coincidence. Sacha and Sara weren't the same names, after all.

'Do you... have a sense about these things?'

Was he trying to make fun of her? He seemed genuine enough, looking her in the eye. She shrugged.

'Is that why you were going to investigate the outbuildings at La Grande Maison?'

The mention of David's house sent a shiver down her spine. Except for the serenity in the abandoned wing, none of the rooms in the château had made her feel one way or another. But in La Grande Maison her emotions had been strong. Had that influenced her curiosity to check out the empty buildings at the bottom of the garden? Or had she really seen a light? Manu seemed to think so.

'Do you think... Have you seen...' What did she want to ask him?

He answered her unspoken question. 'I'm not sure. There's something about those buildings. Unpleasant. I always leave them well enough alone and I'd advise you to do the same.' He glanced around the room with its paintings, its ornaments, and its antique furniture. 'I hope this event won't add another ghost. Do you think Carlier had unfinished business?'

'I think I'll turn in. It's been quite a day.' This was all getting way too freaky. Ghosts were not real. And the people who believed they were, were not like Manu. None of this made sense.

Fortunately, Manu didn't press her. 'Hm. It has. I'll walk you to your room.'

As if she didn't have enough on her mind with a killer on the loose, now Manu had planted ghosts there as well. Though she didn't think the killer would come after her – after all, what would he have against her? – she wasn't entirely at ease either. What if Carlier had been a random victim, and the fact that everyone disliked him had nothing to do with it? Then everyone was fair game.

And ghosts weren't even real. Right? Like Sacha had said, if they were, what could they do? But then, if she were a malicious ghost, she would say that... Maëline hooked her arm through Manu's, glad of his company.

18

Any of us could be bumped off at any moment

I woke to the sound of my phone ringing.

'Wuh?'

'Anyone else dead?'

'Who is this?' Oh. It would be Jacqueline, wouldn't it? 'I don't know, you woke me up. What time is it?'

'Seven thirty. I thought you'd be biting your nails and patrolling the hallways.'

'I thought about it, but I need my beauty sleep.' I rubbed my eyes and tried to collect my thoughts. 'The way I see it, an antler is not a premeditated murder weapon. So unless someone saw something they haven't come forward with, I don't think the killer has any reason to strike again.'

'Unless there was no sane reason in the first place.'

I blinked. I hadn't thought of that. 'Are you trying to scare me?'

Jacqueline sighed. 'I wish we could get there. Forecast says the storm should subside this afternoon. But then, it's always difficult to find good traces in a place such as that, where people are throwing lots of parties.'

'You make it sound like we're having an orgy.'

She let out a frustrated growl. 'With the information we now have, no one could have killed Carlier. Benoît Le Roux was in his room, as attested by Elise, who brought him a drink. The Baillys were in their room together, both running from the other direction, as seen by you. Fabien the magician was with the vicomtesse, and the vicomte was outside checking on the bridge. Three people have no alibi: Sandrine Lardy, who found the body; Romy Martin, who was supposedly on a call to her editor, but he says she wasn't; and Jérémie Gümüs, who was alone in his room but also came running from another direction. But all of them were with others when the body supposedly reappeared!'

'Well, that's one lie you've caught. There must be more.'

'Indeed.' I could hear her teeth grinding. 'See what else you can find out, Julie. We won't be there until at least this afternoon.'

'All right.' I yawned.

'And, Julie?'

'Mmyes?'

'Be careful. I'll call you in an hour.'

'All right. Love you.' Wait, what? I wasn't talking to my mother! But she'd hung up before I could get too embarrassed. So I was embarrassed all through my time in the shower.

I was working my way into my warmest cardigan, which seemed to have shrunk in the wash, when someone knocked on my door. 'You decent?' Beau's voice came through the wood.

'Come in.'

'Not that I would care, but for your own peace of mind.'

'Yeah, yeah. What's up?'

'My one goal in life this morning, *ma caille*, is to escort you to breakfast,' he charmed.

'I will come, but not as your quail. I may not be vain, but I draw the line somewhere. I see you haven't been brutally murdered during the night.'

'You would have heard my manly screams.'

'I'm sure I would.' I knocked on my brother's door, then walked in without waiting for an answer. 'You all right?'

'Wouldn't be very sporting to kill a man with a broken ankle.' David was putting on one shoe.

'I don't think that's the point. Marcel was stabbed in the back. Hm. You think that's significant?'

He shrugged. 'Ask the others.'

'Maybe I should... Jacqueline said the killer could have chosen their victim haphazardly. Good thing I didn't think of that yesterday. Now I have to find out if any of them are psychos.' I shivered, but David pulled up an eyebrow.

'In theory, that could be an option, but then why hide the body and put it back afterwards?'

'See? That doesn't make any sense. Don't you think that supports the theory of a random killing?'

He thought about my words, but then shrugged. 'Not really. Too unpredictable.'

'That's the whole point!' How could he be so cool about this? Contrary to his calm words, I was getting more and more convinced that any of us could be bumped off at any moment.

'Look, Julie, what he means is, there's a difference between picking someone at random to murder them for the sake of it and hiding the body only to put it back later. Those two don't add up.' Strangely, Beau's words made more sense than my brother's. The world had gone mad. But at least I was now back in a state where I could think logically.

'Right. So what we need to do first, is to find out where everyone actually was. Jacquie told me this morning that Romy was not in fact on a call to her editor. So what was she doing in that hallway? To me, that lie has put her on the top of my suspects list. But Corentin and Apolline could easily give each other a false alibi. Elise was very nervous when she told us she brought Benoît Le Roux a drink and she couldn't remember what drink it was. Sandrine was alone, Jérémie was alone – even Manu was alone, both inside and outside. Who says they'll tell us the truth today?'

'He wasn't, though.' Maëline came in after David had answered her soft knock. 'Manu,' she added after seeing my confused face. 'There was an empty coffee cup on his desk, but he only drinks wine and sparkling water.'

'When were you in his office?' David asked. His tone was brusque, but I could tell he was impressed.

'After… I left here. He must have gone outside by then because he wasn't there, but someone else had been in.'

'Yet another lie. I wonder how many more we'll uncover.' Thibault, who up till now had been far too excited at the prospect of catching a killer, seemed more thoughtful today. 'I have to say, it's not as appealing to play detective when you're locked in with the murderer. I wouldn't suspect any of them, ordinarily.'

'How about breakfast first?' I proposed. 'We can have another good look at them.'

David had got the hang of using his crutches, so we got to the dining room at a normal pace. My stomach rumbled at the sight of croissants, *pains au chocolat*, and *brioches aux pralines*. The pink sugary rolls weren't normally something I'd indulge in, but this morning, they looked really good.

Most of the guests were already at the table. The atmosphere was subdued, but not as on edge as the night before. People were talking softly while they ate, and I even spotted a polite smile here and there. They must be relieved at having survived the night. All except Jérémie, of course, but even he seemed less grumpy than the day before. Still, one of them was a murderer.

Or maybe not. The only ones missing were Sandrine and Romy, the person who might have screamed as a distraction, and the liar. A good liar at that – none of us had doubted she was on a call to her editor. On the other hand, a stupid liar, because it could be checked so easily. What else had Romy Martin done that was well executed but stupid?

I sat down next to Apolline and reached for a brioche.

'I thought they would appeal to you. Good morning, Julie, did you sleep well?'

'Apolline. Yes, still alive, thank you. I trust you got a good rest too?' She was the queen of small talk. I had to go through the motions every time I met her in the village. Sometimes twice a day! She still didn't like my business, but she couldn't ignore my money. Annoying? Yes. A killer? I highly doubted it. And an aide to her husband? She couldn't keep a secret if her life depended on it. Which in this case it just might. 'I see Madame Lardy and Madame Martin haven't joined us yet. Do you think they're all right?'

Apolline let out a short laugh while she buttered her croissant. 'Ha! Those two. What would anyone gain from killing them? Martin is a small fish who desperately wants to grow into a shark, but wasn't born to be one. And Sandrine…' Her knife hovered. 'I suppose she's an entry point…' The buttering continued. 'But no use to anyone dead.'

'What do you mean "an entry point"?' I took a bite out of the brioche, the pink praline filling my mouth with a sweetness that called for coffee.

'To Emile, of course. Her husband is probably the richest man in the Beaujolais. Very influential. No wonder Marcel was going after his wife.' The butter squished between her long teeth. Suddenly, my brioche was less appealing.

'Going after? You mean…'

'Of course that's what I mean. What else is she good for? Oh, there you are! Julie, would you mind making room for my friend? How did you sleep?'

What a friend. I hopped over to the next seat, eyeing the thick layers of make-up that couldn't conceal the bags under Sandrine's eyes.

'Now that we're all here,' Vicomtesse Hélène began, 'I'd like to ask you to cooperate with Madame Belmain as she aids the police in their investigation. We start this day without Monsieur Marcel Carlier, and I'd like to take a moment to remember him.' The moment passed very quickly. 'He was an onerous man, but we have to do the right thing and make sure his killer is caught. Thank you.'

Manu, as always at her side, nodded his agreement. He stood and came over to me. 'Is there anything you need?'

'I've been thinking about where the killer could have hidden the body between Madame Lardy's scream and the moment we went in. I'm sure that once we know how, we'll know who. The wardrobe is too small, and there isn't anywhere else to hide in the room. Could there be a secret room or passage or something?'

He laughed at that. 'Believe me, if there was a secret passage, I'd know about it. I played in all these rooms when I was little. Even if you live in a castle, it's still great for the imagination. I pushed all the stones and twisted all the suits of armour. I remember being disappointed every time a new trick didn't work.' His face turned serious. 'In a way, I wish there was a secret passage. Then we could all get out of here, clean up the place, and forget this ever happened.'

Poor man. Walking through the grand corridors and eating breakfast in a room big enough to seat a hundred guests, I could easily forget that this was someone's home. Someone I knew quite well, albeit through my brother. Someone I knew to be very proud of his home and the reputation of his *domaine*. This must hit him extra hard. 'I promise you to do everything in my power to find who did this. I'm sure it won't hurt your business. Might even help it.'

He smiled but didn't seem to put much faith in my words. 'Let me know if you need anything.'

Manu left and David joined me. 'So? Have you had a good look at them?'

'At what?'

'The guests! Our suspects! Manu just told me that there's not only a killer but also a thief on the loose. Several priceless items have disappeared.'

My eyes widened. 'Really? Who would risk killing a person and then drawing more attention to himself by stealing stuff?'

'You think the killer and the thief are the same person?'

I thought about that. I'd automatically assumed so, but why? 'Well... there aren't that many people in our pool of suspects here. What is it – twenty, including staff? What are the odds that they include both a thief and a murderer?'

'They're two very different things, though.'

I ground my teeth. 'Why ask for my opinion, if you're just going to believe the opposite of whatever I say? Go ask Mum instead. She always agrees with you.'

'Oh, like Dad always agreed with you?' He spat the words at me, but the memory of our father made the anger between us crumble. 'You know, I used to envy you for the relationship you had with Dad. But Manu said that fathers aren't always the heroes we think they are. It helped me at the time, but now

I realise we had very different fathers. He still misses his too, though.'

With that, he left me to finish my coffee. Great. Now I was sad as well as worried I might be murdered before the day was done. I'd always been Daddy's little girl. We'd shared a kind of naughty worldview, making fun of the people in our various tribes as though we were on the outside. Looking at the council members from the viewpoint of the churchgoers, and looking at them from the viewpoint of the rambling club. David never understood our bond. To him, people should be respected in their differences, not made fun of. But Dad and I were never disrespectful. Just... observant. Something I would have to be if I were to make it out of here alive.

I took a deep breath to gather all that negativity into one spot, put my fingers to my temple and pulled. I had to pull several times before I could let go of the feeling, but once I had, I felt better for it. Dropping my negativity in the waste basket by the door, I left the dining room to find a quiet spot. I'd realised there was someone else who might like to know about Marcel's demise. She picked up on the first ring.

'Bella, it's Julie.'

'Juliiie!'

I could hear her thinking, which Julie am I talking to? You get used to it, having such a common name. 'I'm afraid I have some bad news. You know Marcel Carlier, the man you introduced me to in Jeanette's café?'

'Oh! Yes?'

'He died.'

She gasped. I know, it was a bit blunt, but they say you shouldn't beat around the bush with bad news, don't they?

'Oh. How? Was it unexpected?'

'I don't think he saw it coming.'

'Wow. That's so... wow. Shame. He said he was going to introduce me to some of his friends. You know how I like to meet new people.'

Yes, as long as they're rich and male. Oops! Time to pull another negative thought from my head. This time I hid it in a suit of armour.

Bella continued, 'Too bad. I was looking forward to that. He had some really good friends, you know? Good people to know, I mean.'

'Hm.' I hoped it sounded acknowledging. Bella didn't make friends unless they could do something for her. That was not the way I operated. 'Do you know of anyone we should inform of his death?'

'Oh, no. I didn't really know him at all. I saw him come out of the Lardys' home, and started a conversation. She's always looking down on me, so I thought I'd steal – I mean share – her friend. He was nice. You know, bit of a bobo, but I can handle them. Like I said, he was going to introduce me... Meh. Anyway, thanks for telling me, Juju. Keep clicking.'

I hated when she said that. But she'd hung up and probably forgotten about both me and Marcel before I could say something. At least she'd confirmed my suspicion. Marcel had been a carrot dangler. It was much more likely that Sandrine had gone to his room because he'd promised her something than because she wanted to be bored together. I should try to talk to her again.

19

Just the place I wanted to be

Thibault joined me on my way back to my room. 'Had a lovely talk with Apolline at breakfast?'

I shuddered. 'I couldn't leave a gap between us. That would have been suspicious.'

'To see her is to take a sudden... chill!' he sang, running his fingers up my back. It made me squirm, which in turn made him chuckle.

'I didn't know you were so Disney-versed.'

'We all have our hidden depths.' He put his hand over his heart, as though he'd said something profound.

'Don't know if I'd call it a depth, but I'll introduce you to my mother.' She was a Disney addict.

'We've met, thanks.' He made a face.

I grinned. 'You're a link to my bad guy ex-husband and you've wriggled your way into my house. She's my mother, she's supposed to be wary of people with the potential to hurt me. But I think she secretly likes you.' I fluttered my eyelashes at him and he huffed, but I caught the little smile around his lips. 'What are your plans for the day?'

'I'm going to stick to Jérémie. Make sure he doesn't do it again. I'll talk to him, play some games or something, find out what he likes, become his friend, and boom! As soon as he confesses, I've got him.'

'I see. You've got it all worked out.'

'Yes, I do. So if you go talk to the others, you can make it seem like we don't suspect him.'

'Oh, thank you for letting me play a part in your scheme.' I made it sound like a joke, but his attitude grated on me. 'Actually, I'd like you to work your magic on Elise. Find out if she really took something up to Benoît's room. She was way too nervous saying that.'

Wrinkling his nose, he gave me the side-eye. 'Work my magic?'

'You know what I mean.'

'There's no magic. She's nice. I can just talk to her. But I don't think I will, if that's how you think of me.'

Wow. Sometimes it was still very obvious he was only twenty-one. Sorry, twenty-two. 'Would you do it for a Scooby snack?'

'I don't feel I'm being treated like a full part of this team.'

'You're not. You're my assistant.'

He gave me a glare. 'You don't pay me to talk to girls.'

'No, that is something you do to *assist* the police. Now will you go talk to Elise, or do I have to?'

'Fine.'

'Fine.' Why was this so hard? Maybe I should send him back to his mother after all. I suppressed an eye roll and he sauntered off.

Jacqueline called. Again. I suppressed another eye roll. 'Hi, Jacquie. I've only had breakfast in the meantime.'

'Talk to anyone?'

'Nothing to report just yet.'

'Okay.' She paused, and I could feel a sense of dread growing in my stomach. 'Would you mind going back to the scene... to Monsieur Carlier's bedroom? We'd like to know where the antler came from, as we couldn't determine this from your photos.'

Ah yes, just the place I wanted to be. Even if he wasn't there any more. But if I wanted to find out *how*, and thus *who*, I'd have to go back to the scene of the crime. I took a deep breath. 'All right. I'll have a look.'

That meant I'd have to ask either Thibault or Manu to help me get in. Unless... I took out my room key and inserted it in the first random door I saw. The lock clicked and the door opened. Jacqueline had already ended the call, so I'd have to tell her later that the locked room hadn't been truly locked after all. In the end, it didn't matter. Even unlocked, the door had been out of sight for no more than a few seconds. The big question remained, where had the killer left the body?

I relocked the door and hurried along the corridors to my room, where I changed into my makeshift crime scene investigation suit – hat, scarf and gloves, and bags to pull over my shoes when I entered the room. By the time I reached Carlier's room, I was sweating heavily. Good thing I'd packed for a week instead of the three days we were supposed to be here.

Now for the moment of truth. I inserted my key and tried the lock. It clicked, and the door opened. A slow clap to my right almost gave me a heart attack.

'Fabien! What are you doing here?'

He strolled down the corridor to my side. 'Good trick. I was wondering if I'd be able to pick the lock, so I came here. Simple curiosity, you see. Bit of a professional challenge, if you will. But I see it required no finesse at all. Still, sometimes the simplest tricks are the best.'

My heart rate slowed to a normal pace. 'The lock isn't the hardest part of this trick. Maybe you can help me work out how the killer did it. As a professional?'

His chest expanded a little. '*Évidemment*. I'm a Jack of all trades! I think that in this case I won't be banned from the guild for explaining how the trick was done.'

'Unfortunately, I can't allow you inside the room. The police will want to search it when they get here. We can't risk contaminating it any more than necessary.'

'Right, right. I don't want to be arrested for something I didn't do.'

'Exactly. So you stay there, while I go in.' As annoying as he was, it might be useful to have a different insight. I walked in and began scanning the walls.

'What are you doing?'

Unless, of course, I had to explain my every move. 'I'm looking for a hook or a hole where a hook might have been.'

'Do you think the room was booby trapped?'

I started to roll my eyes but then stared at him instead. Could he be right? Would someone go to the trouble of rigging an antler to hit a man in the back when no one else was around? It sounded very Indiana Jones to me. But I looked for signs of wires or points of attachment anyway. When I'd gone around the entire room and found nothing, I sighed and turned to the magician.

'No holes, no nails, no recently painted patches. I don't think the antler came from inside this room. Someone must have brought it with them.'

Fabien nodded. 'Not an easily concealed object either, though.' He glanced around the corridor outside the room.

'Nothing here. There's a poster on the opposite wall, but no empty hooks.'

'Ah, yes, the Beau Nouveau,' I said absentmindedly. Aside from the origin of the antler, I was still intrigued with where the body had gone. Was David right, and had Sandrine screamed before there even was a body? That would make her a much better actress than I'd give her credit for.

I opened the wardrobe again, but came to the same conclusion as before – too small. I looked under the bed, but the gap between the bed frame and the floor was less than ten inches. I even opened the little cupboard in between the bookshelves above the built-in desk, though it was four feet off the ground and only measured about fifteen by twenty inches. The ancient wooden knob squeaked when I turned it, but the cupboard itself was empty.

Through all this, Fabien had been talking. I say talking. More like gossiping. He must not even know any of the others very well, but he had his opinions ready. According to him, the whole party had been a fundraiser. Emile Lardy turning down the invitation at the last moment had sent the wrong message to the other investors, who were now rebelling. What against, Fabien never said. But he was sure the party being cancelled would turn out to be a blessing for the owners, not having to feed and wine so many guests.

I'd had enough. 'Okay, shine your light on this. You've stabbed a man in the back with an antler. Someone outside the room screams, so you have very limited time to conceal your crime. It may, in fact, already have been found out. You have a window of a few seconds to flee, but where do you stash the body?'

Fabien stroked his pencil moustache, his gaze roaming the room. 'The wardrobe?'

'Shelves.'

'Under the bed?'

'Too narrow.'

'Behind the tapestry?'

The giant tapestry hung several inches off the ground, but I hadn't thought to check behind it. Stupid! It was the perfect place for a hidden alcove. I stomped over to it, and carefully lifted the antique material off the wall. Bit more. Bit more still. I didn't dare pull the whole thing away from the wall, not to mention the fact that it was immensely heavy. Instead, I slipped underneath, encasing myself between the musty fabric and the bare wall. Creeping sideways in the dark, feeling my way along the rough stones, I eventually emerged on the other side, next to the wardrobe.

'Nothing.' Feeling deflated after my moment of hope, I let my shoulders droop. 'Do you smell something?'

Fabien inhaled rather noisily through his nose. 'Like what?'

'Like...' I sniffed. 'Smelly socks. Stinky feet.' That smell should have gone by now if it had been on Marcel Carlier, as I originally thought.

'Oh. Well, I'm glad I'm not smelling that.'

I sniffed the tapestry, but it only smelled of dust. 'Hm. Gone now.' I shrugged. 'I think I'm done here. Unless you can think of another hiding place?'

'No... If this were a trick, it could involve a number of things. Leaving the body outside the window would be an option if it weren't for the weather giving that away. You've already looked for technical contraptions. Optical illusions would also need some setting up. Besides the timing, of course. You were in here when there was no body, and you were in here when there was a body the second time. The first time could in theory have been an illusion, but how could the killer know that Madame Lardy would look through the keyhole? And then, of course, there's the fact that in that case, the murder would have had to take place at a later time, when everyone was accounted for.'

Huh. He might not be a hero of the sleight of hand, but he seemed to know what he was talking about here. I nodded, locking the door and stripping off all my extra layers.

'Better stop now, or you might get the wrong impression.' He laughed at my eyebrow wiggle. 'Oh, one more thing. You wouldn't know if Jérémie Gümüs's and Benoît Le Roux's rooms are that way, would you?'

'I would indeed. They flank my room on either side.'

That corresponded with them both coming from that direction, then. 'Why didn't you come when you heard the scream?'

'I... had a meeting with Madame Blanc-Mattieu.'

Ah, yes, I'd forgotten. I smiled. 'I'll go put this in my room. If you think of anything else...'

'I'll give the matter some thought,' he promised. 'See you at *déjeuner*.'

As he ambled off, I remembered Beau's words, 'You're a huge flirt'. Perhaps it was true. Franck, my ex-husband, was always jealous. I could never look at, let alone talk to, another man, or he'd get in the way. Come to think of it, he often did that with women too. So now that I was rid of him, I would flirt. I'd flirt with anyone I liked. Yes, part of it was to spite Franck, but mostly, it was for my own satisfaction. Flirting is fun!

As I walked past David's room, a thought struck me. He wasn't much of a flirt. When he liked someone, he really liked them. And boy, did he like Maëline. Why hadn't I seen it earlier? I blamed the murder distracting me, although the signs had been there before. Must be so annoying to like someone you think you shouldn't. I wondered if he felt similarly about me. Much like Maëline, I didn't fit into his world. But underneath all our quarrelling and in spite of himself, I knew he liked me. All the better for him, because he couldn't very well kick me out of his world. As his sister, I was there to stay. Maëline, however, he could still get rid of before he started liking her too much. And the idiot was succeeding.

I had no such qualms about whom I favoured. Everyone I liked would be welcome to stay in my life. And I liked everyone. Well, except for Marcel Carlier, but nobody liked him. And Apolline. And Sandrine. Okay, maybe not everyone.

Fixing my hair and make-up after the indoor hat-wearing, I wondered what to do now. I didn't seem to be any closer to finding out who did it than I was yesterday. My idle hands picked at my nails, and I pulled them apart so as not to ruin my manicure. This is when Henri normally came in for food and a cuddle. He seemed to sense when my hands were empty so he could come and fill them. Poor Henri in the snow. I hoped he'd come in and found a nice warm place on my sofa.

In lieu of a cat to fill my hands, I picked up the bag containing the papers I'd taken from Carlier's room. Using the plastic of the bag, I pulled the sheets apart slightly, so I could have a look without putting my fingerprints all over the papers. Minutes of a meeting, a bill from a printing house, and several printed emails. Well done for considering the environment, Monsieur Carlier. The last page didn't even show anything but the signature. But it did say 'page three of three'. I flicked back to the previous page. One of three.

Whipping out my phone, I started talking before Jacqueline had even greeted me. 'Can you get into Carlier's email?'

'I imagine so, why?'

'He had a printout of one of them, but there's a page missing. Could be relevant?'

'I'm on it. Date and time?'

I gave her the details and told her my findings, or rather the lack thereof, in Carlier's room. I did make sure to mention that anyone could have entered his room – and therefore could also enter mine – with any of the other keys.

'Believe me, Julie, we're doing everything we can to get to you. We're also under pressure from Monsieur Lardy, who doesn't seem to understand that he can't command the weather.'

I couldn't hide a little smile. 'I'll talk to Madame Lardy. See if I can get her to appease her husband.'

With another insistence that I call with every bit of news, she hung up. I supposed I'd better go talk to Sandrine.

I changed my mind when I saw Romy Martin coming down the stairs. She'd lied about why she was where she was at the time of murder, so what had she really been up to in that hallway?

The lights, that were on all the time with the snow blocking out any daylight, flickered. At the same time a draft made me shiver and I hurried towards the journalist.

She halted with her foot still on the last step. 'Madame Belmain, how are you getting on?'

'Oh, I'd rather be taking pictures of bums.'

She laughed. 'If you don't mind, I'd love to write an article about you.'

Bingo. This, I could talk about. It would help take my mind off the thought that if she *was* the killer, I could probably handle her. 'I wouldn't mind that at all. It would help me set the record straight about what I do. When people hear 'pin-up', they immediately think naked ladies, but I don't do nudes. I don't even do lingerie, except for the occasional frilly granny-pants. My ultimate goal is to make women feel good about their bodies, especially if they don't have the standard pin-up silhouette.'

Romy pulled on her pink fluffy cardigan, a reaction I'd seen plenty of women have when thinking about their bodies. Along with a slight pulling together of the shoulders, a tiny wriggle in the seat, tucking a lock of hair behind an ear, and the straightening of a skirt or trouser front, it was a common expression of self-consciousness.

'We all want to be an hourglass, but if you're an apple, just wear a petticoat,' I said with a wink. 'Chocolate chip cookies are too good to skip. Go with the wardrobe tricks instead.'

She laughed again, walking with me towards... Where were we going? She was following me, but I had no idea. Keeping the press happy was in my best interests, so I used my most successful sales pitch and emphasised everything she seemed to react to. In my business, you get to be an expert in body language.

'You should come to my studio. Assuming we ever get out of this castle.'

Romy's pen hovered above her tablet. The draft was stronger here, and I noticed a broken pane of glass in the lead-lights. Little, innocent puffs of snow blew in, slowed, and drifted dreamily down, where they melted in a wet patch on the carpet.

'Does all this get in the way of your work?' I had to get her there somehow.

'Yes and no. This is a much bigger story than it was supposed to be, but I've been told to sit on it. And in the meantime, I can't work on anything else, so...' She shrugged.

'What kind of articles do you usually write?'

Her face twisted. 'Mostly little things. The baker in village X has a new storefront. Fabric shop opening in village Y. The mayor of village Z has been seen buying meat from the supermarket instead of supporting the local butcher. What I'd like to do is the more investigative stuff.' She hesitated, studying my face. Apparently, I had been found trustworthy because she continued, 'I was working on an exposé – high-level corruption in Beaujolais government and business.

Coming here would have been the perfect opportunity for gathering evidence, but...'

'Someone decided to put a stop to the corruption?' If what Romy was telling me now was true, I'd have to find a new main suspect. Though I still didn't know why she'd lied about why she was where she was, if she was working on an exposé on Marcel Carlier, she would have no motive to kill him.

'Indeed.' Her sour look spoke volumes.

'Can I ask what kind of information you had on him?'

She sighed. 'Unfortunately, nothing concrete. Plenty of rumours, but—'

'No evidence. Yes, that seemed to be the theme during the police interviews. Based on your research, though, do you have any... unofficial suspicions?'

Her eyes narrowed. 'Off the record?'

I nodded.

She hesitated, probably weighing her options. Perhaps she needed a bit more incentive. What could I give her that would—

'I know who it's not, if that's any help?'

I raised my eyebrows.

'Benoît Le Roux. Right before the scream, I passed by his room. That server girl, Elise, went in, and he said – well, growled more like – "Give it to me". So, you know, I'll leave it to your imagination what they were doing, but it wasn't killing Carlier.'

Benoît and Elise? I forced my mouth closed. That, I did not see coming. I blinked several times before I could get the thought out of my head. Romy had me with the shock factor, but to be honest, Benoît and Elise were right at the bottom of my suspects list. Along with...

'My brother thinks it's Sandrine. That she screamed only to mislead everyone.'

Romy burst out laughing. 'Oh, that's a good one! Because she used to be an actress? No, I saw her in a play once, must have been twenty years ago, and she was awful. There's no way she could have pulled that off. I was there first, remember? That was genuine shock.'

'Why *were* you there? You could have called your editor from your room.'

'Bad reception.'

'Hm. That doesn't really matter if you're not actually on the phone.'

She held her breath for a second, then frowned. 'I told you, I was gathering evidence. Admitting that I was trying to get into the man's room right after he'd been murdered didn't seem like the most intelligent thing to do. I know lying to the police wasn't either, but... Look, I have no motive here. I've told you before, you should look into Corentin Bailly.'

'Oh, don't worry. We will.' Did I sound like a police person? I felt like a police person. I felt like, if someone would ask 'Who's in charge of this investigation?', I should step forward. But I *might* have been watching too many detective shows since the last murder...

We'd ended up in front of what I remembered from the tour was the library. Romy gave a less than cheerful goodbye. So much for keeping the press happy. I hoped it wouldn't affect my business.

20

I didn't think you were one of them

The thought of Sacha being a ghost would not leave Maëline alone. She knew it was impossible, but before she came to this château, she'd never thought it possible to be involved in a murder, yet here she was.

David sat across from her in the library, staring over the top edge of his book. He hadn't apologised for his last rude remark and had studiously avoided talking about last night. Several times, however, she'd caught him looking at her, now with a frown, then with a faraway, sad gaze. She'd given up trying to make sense of it all. She was here because she was paid to be.

The wind whistled in the ancient chimney, and a puff of soot drifted down.

'Would you mind talking to Sandrine Lardy?' The sound of David's voice made her jump.

'San... Me? Why?'

'The only way that body could have disappeared so quickly is if Sandrine didn't see it in the first place. If it wasn't there before, her accomplice would have had plenty of time afterwards to put it in place. She must be lying.'

Maëline shook her head. 'You weren't there. Julie told me she was genuinely upset.'

'I don't see any other way the killer could have pulled it off. Can you?'

'No, but I thought Julie was the one who was supposed to—'

He cut her off with a frown. 'She can't always be right. She figured it out once, but that's no reason to trust everything she says now. If nothing else, you can help her by talking to Sandrine. Sandrine won't suspect you of trying to work out how she did it. She thinks Julie is on the case.'

'Are you two related or something?'

He looked confused. 'Me and Sandrine?'

Maëline shook her curls. 'No, you and... Forget it. What do you want me to ask her?' She didn't want to talk to the melodrama in seven acts that was Sandrine, but this could be her chance to sneak away and bring Sacha some more food.

David's eyes lit up. If he hadn't been such a jerk, it would have been cute. 'We need means, motive, and opportunity. Means is the antler, opportunity is what she would probably have if she made us think the murder was done earlier than it really was, so what's left is motive. She probably has one because everyone around here had some issue or other with that guy—'

'Marcel Carlier.'

'Right. See if you can find out why she would hate him enough to kill him.'

'Sure. Easy.'

He gave her a glance to assess if she was being sarcastic or not, but she found herself caring less about what he thought. If he terminated her services early, she'd find somewhere else to stay and she wouldn't have to deal with his crotchety behaviour any more. She got up and left the library.

Once outside the room, though, she wasn't sure where to go. Should she talk to Sandrine? Why would Sandrine want to talk to her? Would she be in her room? Where was her room? Ugh, too many questions. Maybe Maëline should head to the kitchen instead and gather provisions for Sacha. The thought had no sooner entered her mind than she'd made the decision and pointed her nose towards the kitchen. At least, she was fairly sure that was where the kitchen was.

For once, she'd been correct in her navigation. The kitchen was a lot busier now, but it was quarter past eleven and lunch would be served at twelve. Maëline glanced around, looking for something she could swipe without anybody noticing.

'Hungry?' Elise flashed her smile, wide and white. 'Don't worry, I won't tell.' She pushed a plate of biscuits over the stainless steel towards Maëline. It would look suspicious if Maëline didn't take one after coming to the kitchen, so she took a tiny bite, eyeing the plate as if it could tell her how to steal it.

'Something on your mind? Other than the murder, I mean. Or is it the murder that has you upset? I didn't think you were one of them.' Elise tilted her head backwards to the rest of the château.

Maëline snorted. 'I'm not. I thought it'd be fun to stay at a château, but now I can't wait to get out of here. I don't know how you can stand to work and be here all the time.'

Elise leaned back. 'Oh, you think I work here? Ha! He wishes. No, we're hired for big events like this, but none of us owe him any loyalty. If it weren't for that bridge, I think most of us would have walked out the moment they found that body. But the chef and the boss told us to keep going, since we are still being paid and, you know, you all had to eat. Can't expect the bobos to prepare their own food, *n'est-ce pas*?' She put on a haughty face that made Maëline laugh.

'That gives me an idea. Can I take these biscuits? I need to go talk to the woman who found the body, and she might be more inclined to see me if I bring goodies.'

Elise pulled up an eyebrow. 'You... *need*... to?'

Maëline sighed and took a bigger bite of the biscuit. They were tasty. 'Fine, they asked me to.'

'So you do it? Are they paying you to?'

'No, but... I'm kind of curious. If what I do will help catch a murderer, then perhaps I should do it.'

Leaning against the steel counter, Elise shrugged, also grabbing a biscuit.

Maëline frowned. 'But actually... She was here, wasn't she? After she screamed, the vicomtesse brought her here, and she stayed until it was time for the presentation in the conference room. Correct?'

Elise shook her head, chewing and swallowing before she spoke. 'No, the old lady brought her here for some tea and cake, but she didn't stay long. The old lady left almost immediately, and the banshee finished her tea and two pieces of cake, but she left long before the presentation was supposed to start.'

That would support David's theory. Oh, how annoying! Not that he could be right. That, she was fine with. But the jolt of pride she felt because of it, *that* took her by unpleasant surprise.

'I suppose I'd better find out what she did in the meantime...' Sacha would have to wait. Unless... 'You said you don't owe Manu any loyalty, so... What if I told you someone inadvertently got locked up in here?'

Elise's eyes rounded. 'Really? The killer?'

'No, no! This person was taking pictures of the abandoned wing when the bridge collapsed. Do you think they would notice if you lent her a uniform?'

'You mean, are they posh enough not to notice the staff?' Elise grinned. 'I don't think we can go that far, but we can hide her in the kitchen. She must be starving. Or has she been living on cheese? Oh, no, wait, that was back this morning. Anyway, would she fit into one of mine? All right, hang on, I have a spare right here.'

Armed with a uniform and a plate of biscuits, Maëline mounted the steps outside the kitchen and turned right. One... two... third door on the right, according to Elise. Knock, knock.

'Who's there?'

'Maëline.'

'Maëline who?'

'Maëline Lamoureux.' Was this a joke? What difference did her last name make?

The door opened to a puffy-faced Sandrine. Red-rimmed eyes stared unrecognisingly at Maëline, then took in the biscuits. 'Those for me?'

'If you want them.'

The door opened further, to let her in. 'Sorry for the mess. It's that stupid reporter. I thought she was being nice, but she kept asking me all these questions about Marcel, when all I wanted to do was forget I was even here. My life is a disaster!'

Big, fat tears dribbled down her cheeks, leaving streaks of mascara. Sandrine flapped her hands towards her face, as if fanning it would dry up the tears.

Maëline held up the plate, feeling sorry for the woman despite the overly emotional display.

Sandrine, though looking down her nose at the biscuits, still took one and gobbled it up. 'You're with Julie Belmain, aren't you?'

Suddenly the urge to contradict the condescending tone in Sandrine's voice was stronger than Maëline's desire to appease. After David's hurtful words, Sandrine's made her feel like nothing more than an appendage, unable to exist by herself, solely there to assist another. Wasn't that exactly what she'd run away from? Before she could get angry, she corrected Sandrine. 'Actually, I came with the owner's best friend.'

The change in Sandrine's attitude was remarkable. She straightened her spine and found a tissue to dab at her eyes. 'Forgive me. It's been a trying couple of days. I'm always so lost without Emile.'

Maëline nodded. 'Have you talked to him yet?'

'Of course! He's quite upset, poor dear. He said he would never let me go somewhere without him again. So I suppose some good has come of it.' She sniffled into her tissue.

'Men.' Maëline could only think of the one word, but it was heartfelt.

Sandrine rewarded it with a watery smile and asked her to sit. 'I mean, it's not like I didn't know anyone. But he knew how much this party meant to me, you know? I was so mad at him, I almost did a very silly thing. But instead...' Her face distorted and she sank back into a crying fit.

Maëline crouched next to her, rubbing her arm and shoulder until she calmed down.

'The worst part is that he predicted it.' The tissue she'd been using was drenched by now, so she took another and blew her nose.

'Who, your husband?'

'No! Marcel! He promised me Emile would notice me again, if I... if we... But then, when I got there, he was... And now Emile *has* noticed me. It's all just so...' She bit her lips and sniffled again. 'Wrong,' she whispered.

David must be mistaken. Could this mess of a woman have pretended to form a liaison with Marcel Carlier, scream to avert suspicion, and then killed him afterwards before attending a presentation? But then where had Carlier been when Sandrine was screaming? Still rubbing Sandrine's back, Maëline tried to find indications of insincerity in Sandrine's behaviour, but she couldn't find any, even with her experience in that field. David *must* be wrong.

'I'd like to be alone now, please.'

'Of course.' Maëline picked up her bundle of uniform but left the biscuits. Sacha would be in the kitchen soon, anyway. It looked like Sandrine needed the biscuits more at the moment.

Every time Maëline turned a corner in this castle, she expected a different view from the one she got. Instead of the corridor with a suit of armour on the right, she found the hallway with the picture of a man on a horse. And though she was sure she had to go up the stairs in the corner opposite, she didn't end up at the stuffed eagle but at the boring corridor with six equally spaced doors. Eventually, though, she had remembered to take the correct exits to all those places and found the curved passage to the abandoned wing.

'Sacha?' she called.

A head appeared at the second door, the room Sacha used for sleeping.

'I got you a uniform. The staff is prepared to hide you.'

Sacha squealed under her chunky scarf and jumped up and down. Then she stormed forward and hugged Maëline.

No ghost, then. Of course she wasn't. But in spite of herself, a tiny bit of Maëline was still relieved.

Sacha changed in under a minute, but Maëline then spent some time trying to convince her to leave her camera behind.

'You'll stand out like a Christmas tree in August.'

'Do you know how much these things cost?'

'But you've been here for days and nobody has come this way. Why would they now come especially to steal your camera?'

'I'm taking it with me.'

Maëline gave up. Sacha led the way back through the line-up of unexpected rooms and corridors, until they ended up at the back of the dining room, and Maëline held Sacha back by the fabric of her sleeve.

'The door is open.'

'I can see that.'

'It's lunchtime. They'll see you.'

'Wasn't it the idea that they'll think I'm one of the staff? What does it matter if they see me?'

Maëline tapped her foot to the ground. 'Your camera?' When Sacha shrugged, she sighed. 'All right, but let me go on the inside.'

Sacha swept her arm through the air in a grand bow to let Maëline go first. They made it halfway across the opening of the double doors before...

'Maëline!'

Pushing Sacha on ahead, Maëline turned towards David, who was coming her way. 'Yes?'

'Anything?' he whispered. Then, frowning, 'Who was that?'

'Oh, just... staff. I did talk to Sandrine, but I don't think she did it.'

'None of the staff have long black hair. They're supposed to wear it tied up.'

Oh. Right. 'Her tie broke?'

David's thundercloud came back with a vengeance. 'Maëline—'

Sacha appeared around the corner with a sigh. 'All right, all right. You've caught me. Girl, you are the worst liar.'

Maëline sighed. 'David, can we keep this between—'

'Who are you?' Julie poked her head around her brother's shoulder.

Maëline groaned.

'This is who you were with?' Coming from David, it sounded like an interrogation. Maëline opened her mouth, but Sacha beat her to it.

'I'm Sacha Toledo. I was photographing the abandoned wing when we all got stuck and I couldn't sneak out. Maëline found me and brought me food. That's all.'

Julie perked up. 'You're a photographer?'

'Kinda. I actually picked it up to get out of a... sticky situation.'

'Nasty relationship?' Julie nodded. 'I know how that feels.'

'Don't we all.' It was out before Maëline knew it. Startled, she glanced at the others. She'd only mumbled it, so perhaps no one had heard.

If she had, Sacha ignored it. 'No, in fact—'

'Let me get this straight,' David said, slightly too loud. Several of the other guests across the room looked up. 'We're trapped in a castle with a killer, and you think it's a good idea to go walking the hallways by yourself, and befriending the one person nobody knows?'

It was too much. 'David!' Maëline burst out. 'I am not a child. I am not an idiot. I can make my own decisions just fine without you commenting on them all the time. What makes you think you have any say in what I do or don't do? Keep your nose out of my business!'

She rammed her shaking hands into the pouch on her jumper. Though she hated confrontation, she forced herself to look up at David. She expected him to be perplexed, or even angry, but instead she was met with a broad grin.

'*Merveilleux.* I knew it was in there somewhere.'

Maëline didn't look, but she knew the other two women were gaping at him as well.

Julie was the first one to speak. 'David, you're an idiot.'

Now he looked perplexed.

'Who do you think you are to assume she'd need you to come out of her shell?'

And there was the anger. David stretched his hand out, indicating Maëline to his sister. 'She's too sweet. If she gets together with Manu, he'll eat her alive. She's never talked back once.'

Maëline blinked. Sacha frowned. Julie opened and closed her mouth a few times.

'Maëline, my brother seems to think you're interested in Manu. Can you please tell him that all you want is a roof over your head until you sort your life out?'

Maëline blinked again. 'How did—'

'What?' David didn't get it either.

'Are you all in some kind of cult or something? I'm not gettin' any of this.'

Julie laughed at Sacha's eruption. 'He's just clueless. He means well, but hey, he's a man.'

'I don't know what your problem is with men, but I happen to like them. And this one's cute. Bit grumpy, but I bet I can make him smile.' She leered at David, who showed an uncanny family resemblance by opening and closing his mouth several times without saying anything. He looked so lost that Maëline took pity on him.

'Julie is right,' she said. 'It is about a man.' She glanced at the other guests, but no one else was listening. Then she stared at the floor while she talked, wringing her hands inside the pouch. 'I met this boy who was crazy about me. My father didn't like him, but he was a... not a nice man. After the way he'd treated me while I cared for him, my father not liking my boyfriend was more of a recommendation than anything else. Then my father died, and I moved in with this boy. He was so sweet, complimenting me on everything. He thanked me for the smallest things I did for him, which was the complete opposite of my father.

'But he got more and more dependent on me. At least, that's what he said. I had to quit my job because he needed me with him at all times. At some point I couldn't even go grocery shopping without him. He was always there. I helped him and comforted him when he thought I was going to leave, and I let him control my life because I believed he needed me. For so long.' She swallowed, forcing back the emotions that came with the memories.

'Until I caught a cold. Then all the sweetness was gone. It was my fault that I was sick, and how was he going to cope without me, and I'd better get well soon because he needed me. But he didn't. And I didn't see it until that moment.'

Maëline rolled her shoulders to get out of the hunch she'd retreated into. 'I took my snotty nose and my bank card with the last bit of inheritance I had left, and I ran. My best friend, whom I hadn't seen in months, gave me the couch to sleep on and helped me get a job.' With her story out in the open, Maëline took a deep breath and looked up. 'You were – are – my first client after I left him. I needed a place to stay, so I tried to be the demure, obedient girl I thought you wanted me to be. Which seemed to work, until Manu showed up.' David froze, and Maëline turned to Julie. 'But how did *you* realise?'

Julie shrugged. 'Looking over your shoulder every time you hear a certain sound. Knowing where all the exits are. Acting a little too casual when the conversation mentions either your personal past or your future... Classic signs. You get through it, though.' She smiled so knowingly and so warmly, it made Maëline tear up. Julie pulled her in for a hug that Maëline needed more than anything. Even just giving the facts of her situation, leaving out the weeks of crying and fear, self-doubt and lethargy, had drained her. Julie's understanding poured a little bit of life back into her.

When she felt strong enough to let Julie go, David was gone. The others filed into the dining room, but Maëline stayed behind, watching them. So now they knew. Would it change how they thought about her?

'I'm...' David had apparently not gone far, but Maëline was not in the mood to talk to him.

'You're sorry, are you? Like the last time you said it? You have a funny way of showing it.'

'I *am* sorry. I know my behaviour has been...'

Why was he searching for a word? There were plenty: horrendous, appalling, disastrous, atrocious…

'Look, I thought you were interested in Manu, and he's a great guy – has a castle and everything – but he's not exactly the monogamous type and—'

'How shallow do you think I am, that I'd go for a guy because he has a castle?' Roof or no roof, she was done dancing to his tune.

'You said he was nice…' He couldn't even look at her any more but he still tried to defend himself. How self-righteous could he be?

'I think a lot of people are nice. Doesn't mean I'm romantically interested in all of them.'

Staring at the floor, he adjusted his crutches. Was he finally out of excuses?

When his gaze found hers again, it was full of misery. 'I said I was sorry. What else can I say?'

'Think about that for a while.'

As she marched past him, she couldn't help but smile. Though it felt a bit cruel to leave him thinking she wouldn't forgive him, he deserved it. For once, *she* would be the one on the high horse.

21

I know one of these people

For me, it was the lack of trust that had taken me the longest to get over. Maëline didn't seem to suffer from that much. As we joined the others at the lunch table and explained Sacha's presence, she and Maëline had so many questions to answer that none of us dwelt on Maëline's story very long. But that slight twinge of envy remained while I worked hard to trust a newcomer to this circle as completely as Maëline did.

True, Maëline had been with this Sacha both before and after the scream, but by her own admission, she'd been lost in the castle for a very long time. Would Sacha have had the opportunity? Did she really not know Marcel Carlier? Was she even a real photographer?

'Would you mind if I have a look at your pictures?'

Sacha grabbed her camera and held it close. Then she considered me and lifted the strap over her head. If all this was a cover story, at least she'd researched her gear. Expensive gear too, for a cover story. But as soon as I saw her photos, all doubt dissolved. She'd captured both the serenity and the sadness of past glory so well that I found myself longing to visit these rooms. The mossy curtains, dusty shelves, and ragged wall silk told their own story of opulence and decay. Mesmerised and delighted, I looked up to see Sacha smiling wide.

'Wait till you see them edited. I go way dark on exposure, reduce saturation, and lower my temperature. You get that gritty, haunting look.'

I nodded, following her changes in my head. I wasn't sure I'd like those edited pictures better than the originals, but to each her own.

'By the way, I know one of these people.' She turned her back on them and looked me in the eye. 'That reporter? Romy Martin. She's ruthless. Cracked down on some of my buddies. Made it look like we were destroying things. But our pictures show how careful we are not to disturb anything. Anyway, she got what she wanted. They were charged with trespassing and told not to enter any more abandoned properties. And what was in it for her? One story maybe?'

What some people will do for a story. I glanced along the table at Romy, now in animated conversation with Corentin Bailly, who'd said those exact words. But to me, Sacha was still the newcomer.

'How did you get into the castle? You know how to pick locks?'

Sacha burst into tinkling laughter. 'No! I'm not a criminal. When I came, there wasn't all that much snow yet. People were coming and going all the time, cleaning and stuff. Nobody ever notices me. Once inside the outer wall, you can go around the part of the château they still use. It's a bit of a trek through nettles and brambles, even in winter, but once you're there, you have your pick of broken windows to use. I only went into the house because I was really hungry. Did Maëline tell you about the men in the kitchen?'

'What men?' Who else was roaming these halls without anyone noticing? The way this was going, none of my suspects had killed Carlier. He'd been hidden by mysterious men in the night.

'Two nights ago, yeah? I'd been trapped already because the snow made my original entrance too dangerous to use. So I thought I'd go through the castle, even though that's, like, real trespassing. And I get to the kitchen, right? Okay, so I know I shouldn't have, but I was real hungry, so I thought I'd get some food before sneakin' out. In the dark, there were these three guys with torches. They were in and out of the fridge a few times, mumbling to one another, but I couldn't hear what they were saying. Freaked me right out! I thought, if they're burglars, what are they stealing from the fridge? Unless, you know, that's where they keep the ice.' She showed me the tip of her tongue in a big grin.

I smiled, but not very heartily. This was the night before the bridge went, so they were probably long gone. Still, the thought of the château being burgled so shortly before the murder seemed more than a coincidence. On the other hand, Sacha had a point. What could they possibly have been looking for in the fridge?

The vicomtesse joined us on Sacha's other side, asking her what this 'urbex' was. When she realised what Sacha had been doing, she launched into a comprehensive history of the château that had my ears bleeding in no time. Sacha seemed interested enough for us both, so I focussed on my dessert.

'Alone at last.'

Beau's voice made me jump. 'What have you been up to?'

'I'll tell you. Never been a fan of *canelés* anyway.'

Admittedly, the little pastries often had an almost squeaky chewy texture, but these were yummy. How much rum was in them?

'I'm still convinced it was him.'

Yum, rum. 'Who was that, again?'

'Jérémie. I told you he did it.'

I looked up. 'You have proof?'

His confidence crumbled. 'Well, no... but hear me out. While you went off looking for clues, I already knew who did it, so I kept watch on Jérémie. And it paid off. He had a very secret meeting with Corentin Bailly. Watching over his shoulder all the way to the room, locking the door, that sort of thing. But he didn't realise I could easily hear him from outside, as he didn't bother to keep his voice down. He was pretty desperate, too, by the sounds of it.'

History must not have witnessed much intrigue in this château. Overhearing things was far too easy. Thibault was loving it, though. He recounted his tale with a light in his eyes and plenty of gesturing.

'What Corentin said, I couldn't really hear, but Jérémie said he'd counted on a grant that now had gone to something called La Tisseuse and asked if Corentin could put a stop to it. Apparently he couldn't, because Jérémie burst out about Corentin being useless and letting local businesses down even after the main obstacle had been removed. One guess for what, or rather who, he meant by that.'

'Tweedy—' I winced. I hadn't liked the man, but Maëline was right. I should at least show him some respect. 'Marcel Carlier,' I obliged.

'Bingo! He went on and on about how much he hated him and that he was responsible for the downfall of Jérémie's *domaine*. In the category Motives, Jérémie wins.'

'But he did come running from the direction of his room. I think I'll ask Benoît if he saw him actually exit his room. If not, he might have done that U-turn you're in favour of. But that still leaves us with the mystery of the missing body. I keep thinking that once we know how, we'll know who.'

'Not necessarily.' Manu had left the table and had apparently picked up my last words on his way out of the dining room. 'We only have Madame Lardy's word for it that there was a body there the first time. Even if she didn't commit the murder, could she have been working together with someone?' Then he raised his hands in front of him and shook his head. 'I'm sorry. Everybody here is my guest. I don't want to cast suspicion on anyone.'

With that, he left the dining room, but Beau and I looked at each other.

'Jérémie?'

'Romy?'

We said the names at the same time. I bit my lip in thought. If my brother was right, and Sandrine was working with someone to screw up the timeline, it could be anyone.

My phone beeped in my pocket. Jacqueline had forwarded me the email, including the missing page. One word in the body text: *interesting*. While Thibault followed Jérémie out of the dining room, I scrolled down to the original email on my way to the conference room.

As much as I hated to admit it, this page proved that Marcel had played a part in the bankruptcy of Jérémie's business. As motives go, it was a good one. But was it enough? I sighed, connecting to the printer so I could provide my suspects with something tangible. First stop, Rodent McRatface.

Thibault was loitering outside Jérémie's room.

'Anything exciting happen?'

He shrugged.

'You were right.' I waved the sheet of paper. 'Jérémie is bust. Partly because of Marcel.'

He pumped his fist, then pointed his finger at me. 'Ha! See?'

'It doesn't prove he killed him.'

'Let's ask him, then.'

'My thoughts exactly,' I said with a knock on the door.

It took Jérémie a while to open the door, but as soon as he did, Thibault asked, 'Did you kill him?'

Jérémie paled. 'Is that what the police think?' The pale turned grey. 'Of course they do. It makes sense, doesn't it.' It wasn't even a question any more. He stepped aside to let us into the room.

Beau made a beeline for the desk, but I remained near the door so I could face Jérémie, who slouched on the edge of the bed.

'You have a very good motive.' I showed him the email, but he kept staring at his shoes.

'I know I do. I had every reason to hate him and I did. But I didn't kill him.' He looked me in the eye when he said that. Then he went back to shoe-staring.

'Where were you at the time of the murder?' I felt very police-y again, asking that.

'I told you, I was in my room when Madame Lardy screamed. I returned there until it was time for the presentation. I almost didn't go. But that would have made me even more suspicious, wouldn't it? Everybody there knew that my business was struggling. I don't even know why Monsieur Blanc-Mattieu invited me. But – of course – I held my head up high and I went.'

'Can you prove that you were in your room?'

'No.'

'Can anybody else verify it?'

'No.'

'Is there any reason why we should not see you as the main suspect?'

He remained silent for so long that I was trying to come up with another question, but then he said, 'I... overheard... a conversation between Marcel Carlier and... The other person stormed out of his room, saying, "I'll make sure you get what you deserve". It was... Benoît Le Roux.'

Beau and I exchanged a look. This was new information to both of us. 'Thank you. That was most helpful.'

'You... you're not going to arrest me?' Jérémie's face was utter confusion. 'But I thought—'

'We are not the police, Monsieur Gümüs. We're only helping them find a killer. Whether or not that's you remains to be seen.'

'But you might want to come clean about the redecorating you have planned.' Arms folded, Thibault leaned against the desk. When neither Jérémie nor I moved, he pointed at the suitcase at the foot of the bed. It wasn't entirely closed, but from what I could see, only clothes spilled out.

Jérémie, however, jumped up and tried to close the suitcase, stuttering as he worked. 'That's just a little... thing that I... picked up from... to give to... I mean, I could...'

'You mean you should put it back where it came from. I don't think our host would look kindly on you taking his heirlooms.'

'Right. Right,' Jérémie said, making no effort to open the suitcase.

Beau decided it was time for a little power play, standing up straight with fists on hips. The suitcase flew open, revealing a massive antique silver chalice. It might not save Jérémie's business, but it could probably send him on a comfortable holiday.

Jérémie regarded it with no small amount of regret. 'Would you mind... If I put it back when no one is looking... can we keep this between us? I've never done anything like this. But faced with all this wealth, I...'

He scrubbed his face with his hand, leaving it over his mouth while he stared at the chalice.

'If... it has no further bearing on the case?' I wasn't sure how Thibault would react to my softheartedness, but he nodded. 'We will make sure it's back where it belongs before you go.'

'And also whether you haven't been tempted by the wealth again,' Beau added.

Jérémie nodded curtly, and we left.

'Well spotted!'

He gave me a sideways grin. 'I had good training.'

Not from me, he hadn't. But that was probably why his family wasn't 'officially' criminal. Except, of course, from my ex-husband.

As we approached the door to Benoît's room, it opened, and out stepped the giant.

'Monsieur Le Roux, I have a question for you. Do you have a minute?'

'For you, always,' he boomed, his eyes twinkling. Then his gaze fell on the email I still held in my hand, and the twinkling stopped. 'It's not what you think.'

Oh. Probably not, then. What I had been thinking was to ask him if he'd seen Jérémie come out of his room after Sandrine's scream, but this should be interesting too. 'Explain it to me, then.'

Beau performed his broad stance again behind me, but aside from doubting whether it would have impressed as big a man as Benoît, I didn't need the back-up. Benoît sighed and let us into his room. Behind his back, Beau raised his eyebrows at me, and I discreetly held up my palms.

'It's not her fault. I asked her to help, and she thought it would be, err... a cool spy mission, or some such thing, is what she made of it. She's almost an innocent bystander. Certainly not a killer.'

Who was he talking about? Oh, wait! I knew that. 'We don't think Elise killed anyone.' Behind Benoît, Thibault's jaw dropped. Point for me. 'But we'd like to know exactly how she helped you.'

'Well...' Benoît rubbed his neck with a gammon of a hand. 'She didn't even, really. I asked her to sneak into Marcel Carlier's room during lunch and try to find me some evidence of his illegal practices.' The already considerable volume raised more. 'I *know* he's skimming money from the organisation. The bills he sends us for glossy printed flyers are exorbitant. Or... they were.' He calmed at the realisation. 'Anyway, Elise was happy to help me catch a criminal, as it were, and so she brought me this.' He gestured towards the email in my hand. 'It was certainly a shady deal, but nothing illegal, as far as I could see. And it had nothing to do with the Comité d'Histoire et du Patrimoine du Beaujolais, so it didn't help my investigation. I suppose it doesn't matter now. Unless you suspect Elise.' The volume rose again, and I fought the urge to cover my ears. 'In that case, I'll have to strongly—'

'Elise is not a suspect! At least, not as far as I know. We are, of course, not officially with the police.'

Benoît nodded, appeased for now.

'So, what I wanted to ask... Did you see Jérémie Gümüs come out of his room when Sandrine Lardy screamed?'

His eyebrows lifted. '*That's* what you wanted to ask? Let me think... Yes... Yes, I was already past his door when it opened and he asked what was going on. Absolutely. Yes. He was in his room.' He nodded to underline his words, and the twinkle returned.

I left the room feeling deflated. 'I don't know, Beau. Everybody has a motive, nobody has the opportunity. Option one – Marcel Carlier was dead when Sandrine screamed and he disappeared into thin air. Or option two – Sandrine was working with someone, but nobody was out of sight for long enough afterwards to kill him. Also, where was Marcel at the time of the scream? And lastly, that would make the antler a premeditated weapon. Where did it come from?'

Thibault scratched his chin but didn't have any brilliant ideas. Or even far-fetched ones.

'I'll be in my room. I need to think.'

Once there, I dropped onto my bed. I missed Henri. Somehow, he always knew when to show up so that I could sit and pet him like an evil overlord and think. Thinking works best when stroking warm fur. At least the storm had finally subsided, so it looked like we might not have to stay much longer. Imagining the poor furball in the cold almost made me cry and I grabbed my phone to stare at his picture.

The first photo that came up, though, was the Beau Nouveau. Ugh, show-off. I'd already swiped past his picture, when I realised what I was looking at. This was outside the crime scene, not long before the crime took place. We'd even met Carlier there. Aside from the murderer, we might have been the last people to see him alive. Unfortunately, the photo didn't give me any clues as to who else could have been near. But... there was something. A reflection in the glass protecting the poster. I magnified the section. The antler!

Dropping the phone to my lap, I stared at the canopy. So it *was* a weapon of convenience. Did that rule out a later murder? Was Sandrine's distress genuine? In theory, the murder could have been committed earlier, Marcel's body dragged to another room, then Sandrine could have screamed, and the body could have been replaced when everyone was somewhere else. But that was just it. Afterwards, everyone was with someone else. And why replace the body at all? Why draw attention to it by screaming?

I pressed my fists to my eyes. None of it made sense. Before I started theorising, I'd been convinced Sandrine's hysteria was real. I'd only doubted it because it made the most sense if she was in on it, but if she wasn't... there *must* be a secret passage of some sort. But where would it g—oh. Oh!

I jumped up and raced to the next room. 'Maëline?' No Maëline. One door further. 'David?'

'What's going on? Has someone else been murdered?'

'No, but I know who did it. Get everyone together in the library. I'm going to call Jacqueline.'

He grinned. 'Looks like you're having a Poirot moment.'

When I entered the library, it contained only David, Beau, Romy, Benoît, Hélène, and Fabien.

'Where are the others?' Poirot never had this problem.

David counted on his fingers. 'Jérémie didn't want to be accused again. Apolline and Corentin said they'd hear about it later. And I texted Manu and Maëline because I couldn't find them. He's outside, checking on whether they can start rebuilding the bridge, and she hasn't answered.' Mumbling, he added, 'I think she's ignoring me.'

22

Stay away from her!

Where was she? Maëline knew she had a bad sense of direction, but this castle threw her off track with every corner she turned. She must have passed this corridor with the big window at least five times. With a sigh, she relented and leaned against the window sill. Now that the wind had stilled and only a last few snowflakes twirled down from the sky, the outside world had a calming effect. Soft and pure, the snow seemed to say, 'All will be well'.

At least she didn't have to pretend not to have opinions any more. The words to relate her story had come out more easily than the emotions attached to it. Maëline pressed her eyes closed. It would be a while before she could tell the story without needing some quiet time afterwards. David's presence hadn't made it easier. And to think that he'd meant to protect her! Who needs a knight like that? Annoy her into losing her temper. That'll help her in life.

With a sigh, she pushed away from the window and picked up her wanderings. He'd been so much fun that first morning. Couldn't they go back to that? Something crunched under her shoe, and she halted. A rusty nail? Where had that come from? The vaulted ceiling looked pristine, as did the plastered, white walls. But the wood of the door frame was dried up and cracked. With nothing better to do, she stepped up to the wood and examined it. Aha! But how did it get from the door frame to the middle of the corridor carpet? Especially if there was nothing hanging off of it.

She was still contemplating this little mystery when a sound came from within the room. Wasn't everyone supposed to be in the library? Perhaps someone else, like her, had taken the opportunity to have a moment by themselves. She was about to leave them in peace and continue down the corridor when she remembered Sacha's ghost-in-the-walls. Did this sound like a ghost?

Curiosity got the better of her. A tiny little peek through the keyhole wouldn't hurt anyone. She knelt down and squinted through the little hole. Someone was moving around a big object. Against the light in the background, she couldn't make out much, but shouldn't an object of that size be much heavier?

A large hand clamped over her mouth from behind, stifling her scream. After half a second of tensing up, she turned around, ready to attack or defend or whatever was needed. Hands raised like claws, she paused at the sight of David holding his finger to his lips. Dropping her hands to her sides, she relaxed her posture but kept a safe distance. Why was *he* here? Why was he *here*? Why did he want her to be quiet when his last words had been to encourage her to speak up?

Speak up, she would! She opened her mouth, but he closed the distance between them and put his hand over her mouth again, gently pushing her away from the door and down the corridor.

'Come with me. Now!' he whispered.

'What—?' she hissed, but he picked up his crutches and kept pushing, even when someone behind them shouted.

'Dav! Maëline, hold up.'

Cursing his crutches, David stepped in front of Maëline and turned to his friend. 'Stay away from her!'

A puzzled smile spread across Manu's face. 'What? Look, I know you're still sore about that girl from years ago, but...'

'That's not what I'm talking about, and you know it. But if you just come with me—'

'Don't take me for granted! I'm sick of people thinking they know me!'

Maëline jumped at Manu's angry outburst. She tried to get a better look at Manu, but David kept stepping in front. Was he being an unnecessary knight again?

Manu didn't seem to understand either, from the glances Maëline caught of him. He took a few steps forward, but David stepped back, pushing her along with him.

'It won't work, Manu. There's two of us now.'

He couldn't mean…? Maëline stared at the back of David's head, trying to look inside. How had he gone from suspecting Sandrine to accusing Manu? His friend Manu! She backed up a little but bumped into someone else.

A strong arm kept her from falling over. Thibault flashed her a small smile, but quickly refocussed his attention on Manu, whose gaze flicked from David to Maëline to Beau and on to Julie, who appeared around the corner, panting slightly.

'I would never hurt you, David. You or Maëline. I should hope you would know that.' Manu's shoulders drooped. 'But I did hurt… I k—' He sobbed. He buried his face in his hands, standing by himself in the middle of the corridor, until the vicomtesse pushed through and hugged him. He held on to her slight figure as if to a lifebuoy.

'She… knew?' Maëline felt as if she'd skipped a few chapters. None of this made sense.

Julie nodded. 'She's the one who put the body back.'

23

Weren't you scared?

The police finally managed to make their way to the château. By then, all the guests had retreated to their rooms to pack. Beau and I had taken Manu to the *petit salon*, where he'd sat all this time with his face in his hands. David and Maëline had come with us, and the vicomtesse had not left her son's side. Sitting next to him on the settee, with her arm around him, she now told Jacqueline all she knew, including her guests by looking at each of us in turn.

'I partly blame myself,' she began.

At this, Manu lowered his hands and shook his head, but she cut him off before he could speak by placing her free hand on his arm.

'I shied away from the world after my husband died and left my son to deal with all the mess. I tried to help, but... Oh, I was so proud of him. All the clever ways he found to make us more money. While everyone around us put no faith in him at all, he kept us afloat.' The affection with which she stroked his hair was almost painful to watch, knowing what was coming.

'But it wasn't enough. Without the support of the community, we weren't going to make it. After my husband had committed the unforgivable sin of selling to a foreigner – an American in this case – we were persona non grata. Manu had no choice but to turn to that same American for help, but... Something had changed. I'm not exactly sure what happened, but I knew something was wrong when Manu didn't want to discuss this business deal with me when he'd always done so before. I heard him muttering about the cheese Mafia one time, and he deliberated on this deal for quite some time. At some point, though, he cheered up, and I assumed he'd made a decision.'

She turned to her son. 'I'm sorry, *chéri*, but I don't think it was the right one.'

Still staring at the carpet, Manu shook his head. 'Devereaux, the American my father had sold to, saw my desperate situation. He turned out not to be the straight businessman my father had taken him for. He offered me a deal in exchange for my help smuggling French cheese into the United States.'

With pleading eyes, he turned to his mother. 'I just didn't see any other way out.'

She replied with a hug and continued stroking his back when he finally looked at Jacqueline. 'It worked for a while.

Nobody suspected a thing, and we were finally in the black again. I applied for several grants, and if I could have brokered this last one with the Comité d'Histoire et du Patrimoine du Beaujolais, I could have left the smuggling operation, and nobody would have been any the wiser. But Carlier suspected something. He didn't know what it was, but he demanded a cut or he would go public. Even without evidence or concrete accusations, his word as an expert alone could have ruined everything.

'After lunch yesterday, he came to my office. He said he wouldn't ask for his cut because he already knew the answer, so I could tell him whenever I was ready to accept. With those words, he left the office. I racked my brain for ways out of this situation but couldn't find any, so I followed him to his room to try and reason with him. Carlier, however, had no intention of relenting. I was already on my way out, when Carlier said that my mother must be exceptionally timid or stupid to not only have married a man with no business sense, but also to leave an incompetent son in charge. That's when I lost it. I ripped the antler from the door frame and charged at him.'

Henri was on my lap. I was on a couch that had been scratched beyond all recognition. Outrage had fought with relief, but one touch of that furry head and relief had won. So I covered the couch with a *jeté de canapé*, which had the added bonus of being nice and fluffy, and cuddled the cat senseless.

My friends were dying to find out what happened. I'd had to call Maile because she didn't want to risk the roads just yet, but Tiana and Céline were here with me, sipping hot coffee and hanging on my every word. When I got to the point in the story when Jacqueline asked Manu to follow her, Thibault got up to answer the door, and I could hear Maëline stomping the snow off her boots.

'Hi, everyone, sorry I'm late.' Her rosy cheeks round with a smile, she introduced herself. Both Tiana and Céline tried to keep from gaping but failed miserably.

'Did my brother give you any trouble?'

Maëline laughed and shook her curls. 'He's so considerate, it's funny. I know I shouldn't take advantage of him, but...'

I waved her reserve away. 'He has something to make up for.'

'He said I could stay for as long as I wanted. That's worth a lot to me right now. And I felt I had to apologise to him, too, for getting almost caught by a murderer right after he'd told me it was a silly thing to go roaming the hallways.'

I frowned. 'He's not treating you like a porcelain doll, is he?'

She smiled again. 'Don't worry, Julie. He's back to being nice. It's actually quite freeing to have my story out in the open. No more pretending.'

'And if you do need to talk, you know where to come.'

'I'm sorry to change the subject, but weren't you scared?' Tiana examined Maëline as if she were an artefact in a museum.

'Oh! No... I actually didn't realise Manu had killed Monsieur Carlier until he admitted it himself.'

'But you figured it out,' Céline said to me. I opened my mouth to answer, but Beau cut in.

'The problem was that everybody had a motive. Even Elise, who didn't know him, had already met his ugly side when he accused her of spilling coffee on him. Not that that's a reason for murder, but he had a habit of making people dislike him, to say the least. He charged too much for printing committee flyers, he destroyed reputations, he arranged memberships for some while barring others... I think the only one we didn't suspect was the magician.'

'Though he did know how to pick a lock.'

Beau snorted. 'Hardly a lock, that. Anyway, there was another problem. None of the people with all the beautiful motives had the opportunity. We had seen Carlier not long before Sandrine screamed, so it had to have happened fairly quickly. Unless... Sandrine screamed for nothing because she wanted to make us think the murder happened earlier than it actually did. But everybody was accounted for after her scream, so that couldn't be it either.'

'Except Sandrine herself.' Everyone stared at Maëline. 'Elise told me she didn't spend all that much time in the kitchen after the vicomtesse brought her. So in theory, she could have done it.'

Thibault looked at me and laughed. 'Good thing we didn't know that!'

I huffed. '*We* may not have known that, but *I* had other evidence to go by.' Who'd solved this crime, anyway? Him and his 'we'. 'I took this picture of Beau' – I showed them all my phone, while Beau took on the same pose as in the picture – 'and as you can see' – I enlarged the reflection – 'the antler is still on the wall outside. That proved it was a weapon of convenience, which made the idea of Sandrine or anyone else coming back to finish the job very unlikely. Though not impossible, of course. But if the murder had occurred when Sandrine saw it, where had the killer left both himself and the body?

'There had to be a secret passage. And the only person who could possibly know about that was Manu. But there we had the next problem. Manu was with other people from the moment we all came together in front of Carlier's room. And why put the body back at all? Why not leave it in the passage until everyone had gone?

'It wasn't until I thought about where the passage could lead that all the pieces fell into place. From the medieval saint appearing in the village when he was also at the castle, to the stinky feet smell. Carlier's room was in a tower that was one of the oldest parts of the château. Manu had told me himself that he spent his childhood looking for secret passages and that if there was one, he'd know about it. He never denied there was one. I hope Maurice did other things to deserve his sainthood because he clearly wasn't in two places at once. Though that story did fool me. I thought the passage would lead all the way to the village of Saint-Maurice. Manu told us that it did, in fact. But there was also a side entrance that led to the courtyard. Manu had come from outside, but the only snow on his coat came dripping from his hair. He had to have put it on after he came back in. That's also why he changed his jumper. It had soaked up the melted snow.'

'A secret passage? That's a bit of a let-down. I thought it'd be cleverer than that,' Tiana said over the rim of her coffee cup.

'It was a good one, though. The whole wardrobe swung open if you turned the knob on the cupboard on the other side of the room the wrong way. No wonder it took him so long to find. But you know what? If that's not good enough for you, next time we have a murder in a locked room, I'll phone you.'

'Yes! Do!' She grinned.

Céline held up her palm. 'But what about the mother?'

'It's her castle, *non*?' Beau said. 'She knew about the passage and so she suspected it was Manu. He'd been off the straight and narrow before, but this was too far.'

'What do you mean?'

He was hijacking my story again. But Céline's unveiled admiration kept me quiet. For now.

'Remember the stinky feet? Manu had to fill us in on this because even Madame Smarty Pants couldn't work that one out.'

Keep quiet, Juju...

'As it turns out, the wine wasn't bringing in enough for the upkeep of the castle, so despite everything Manu had tried – and he'd done some pretty smart things – he had to find other ways of making money. Some American smugglers offered him the chance to import his wine to the US legally, if he'd help them out with some less legal cheese deals. Ordinarily, he'd buy up the cheese and store it in the fridge, then his henchmen would take it out in the middle of the night and take it to their storeroom. Through the secret passage. You'll never guess where it ends up.' He paused for effect, which only made his exclamation more triumphant. 'In her big, fancy family mansion!'

'Well, the empty outbuildings.' He made it seem like my family was in on this shady deal.

'That's why I saw the spooky light,' Maëline said.

'And why I got that snow dumped on me when I got too close. Did I tell you they tried to run over me with their van? Jacqueline added that little mishap to their charges,' I added with no small amount of satisfaction. 'So that's how we all ended up in the castle in the first place because my brother told Manu over the phone that he was going to check on the outbuildings later. Manu couldn't risk his friend discovering the illegal cheese, so he invited us over.'

Tiana looked as if she was doing a difficult sum in her head. 'So... did they take the wrong cheese?'

'They did!' It was all an elaborate joke to Beau. 'The night Sacha saw the men in the kitchen, they took the cheese that was meant for the guests. They weren't supposed to be there, but they hadn't got the memo.'

Céline wore a frown on her pretty face. 'I still don't see how the mother fits in.'

Thibault, expert on mothers, took it upon himself to explain. 'She knew what Manu was up to. I mean, she never leaves that castle, so you better believe she knows what goes on inside it. But she also knew she'd lose her home if she said anything about it. So she stood by and let it happen. When a murdered man disappeared, however, she couldn't let that pass. She brought Sandrine to the kitchen, returned to the scene of the crime, and took Marcel Carlier out of his hiding place. Her intention, she told us later, was to make Manu come clean, but he thought he could still get away with it.'

Pressing Henri to my chest, I kissed his furry head. 'In a way, I feel bad for Manu. He lived in the shadow of his father's bad decisions. Whatever business choices he made, people took it for granted that he would fail too. He said that's why he turned to foreigners. The locals had given up on him before he ever got started.'

We all let that sink in. I wondered if they ever talked to him about his 'little business', feeling sick as I thought of Apolline and the way she left that château as if she'd stepped in something nasty.

Céline was still trying to work out something else. 'But how did you know it was her?'

'Partly because it was the only logical solution, but also, when I went to get her to come to the presentation, I stood in a wet patch outside her door., I realised later that, rather than another maintenance issue, it was melted snow. Hélène didn't have a spare key to that room and she couldn't risk anyone seeing her enter a suspected crime scene. So she had to go around via the secret passage. They must have had some of the cheese stored in the passage as well because I noticed a smelly grease stain on her skirt.'

'I'm still a bit disappointed there weren't any ghosts involved.' Maëline winked. She did seem lighter after telling her story and realising nobody pitied her. And David offering her one of his twelve rooms was no more than logical.

Thibault burst into laughter. 'I can still see Sacha's face when she cried, "So you were the ghost in the walls!" Priceless!'

Maëline laughed as she got up. 'I'd better get back. We've opened the gates so the children can use that perfect slope for sledging. It's amazing to watch their happy faces.'

I could almost feel my jaw drop. Those gates had been firmly shut for as long as I could remember. We weren't even allowed to sledge there ourselves when we were little. David had been on the conservative side since he took over the house, but all it took was one Maëline. File that for future reference.

'Have fun,' I said, instead of 'welcome to the family'.

Céline also had to get back to the bakery, so Beau let them both out, putting some more emphasis on how *we* had found another killer.

Tiana noticed my change in temper. 'You don't seem to like the fact that you like him.'

I grunted. 'No, he's all right. What I don't like is that he takes me for granted. He doesn't appreciate that I'm his boss.' Oh. Was that it? Huh.

Tiana giggled. 'Right. I'm going to leave you with that. If you want, I got you that ticket for the Beaujolais Nouveau concert tonight. Think about it. See you later, Juju.' She kissed both my cheeks and left, just as Thibault came back into the room.

'Beau...' I pushed Henri off my lap and ambled to the big cupboard in the corner where I kept my stash. I handed him two picture frames. As expected, he stared at them. As unexpected, he turned bright red. 'I know it's custom in your family to take things, but if you want to continue to live and work here, you have to understand that I am your employer. My things are not your things. I pay you to buy those things for yourself if you want them.'

He cast his gaze down.

'But as your friend, I want you to take these to frame your art.'

When he glanced up, I wasn't sure what to make of his intense look. But it passed and transformed into a wide smile. 'You're all right, *ma crevette.*'

'I am not your shrimp!'

Other books by Christa Bakker

<u>*Other books in this series:*</u>

Death by Naked Ladies

Beaujolais Blood

The Cold Case: a Vintage Murder

Sign up for a FREE Christmas story at

<u>https://christabakker.com/newsletter</u>

Acknowledgements

I'm so grateful for everyone supporting me in this journey. Firstly, there's my editor, Kristen Tate with The Blue Garret. Without her, my stories wouldn't sparkle the way they do.

My mother and my friend Carole Marples have been good enough to read my sloppy writing and tell me how to improve. Believe me, I needed it! Thank you both so much!

Nienke Grasset of La Tisseuse has been invaluable in correcting my pigeon French. *Merci!*

And my long-suffering husband can breathe easy now that another book is done. Thank you so much for the support! Now go make me a sandwich, darling.

Editing by Kristen Tate at The Blue Garret

Book cover by Christa and Erik Bakker

1st edition 2023

ISBN: 978-1-8383181-6-1

Visit the author's website at: www.christabakker.com